the Trouble with Christmas

loren sorensen

Cover Illustration by ollie_creates

1st edition November 2023 | 2nd edition December 2024

Ebook ISBN: 979-8-9892975-3-5 | Paperback ISBN: 979-8-9892975-2-8

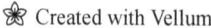 Created with Vellum

To those who doubt their own strength and struggle to accept love: Never forget that you are enough and worthy.

Even in the darkest days that light still shines.

author's note

T he *Trouble with Christmas* is a novella that builds the foundation of a romantic relationship between two secondary characters from the first book in my True Heart Series, *Love in Plane Sight*. Caleb is Isla's younger brother, and Rayanne is Isla's best friend. Their love story begins here, but it doesn't conclude with a happily ever after...yet. Rayanne and Caleb have a hell of a story to be told, and it all starts here. For the first time ever, this second edition offers an extended epilogue that follows the ending of *The Trouble with Christmas* when Caleb and Rayanne exchange Christmas presents.

Please note that the image for Caleb's Chapter Heading is sfogliatella, an Italian pastry that plays an important role in the story.

You, the reader, are important to me, as is your mental health. I've compiled a list of Trigger Warnings and ask that you consider each item's impact on your well-being before continuing. The following list is including both *The Trouble with Christmas* and the second epilogue, *The Trouble with Presents.* While the detail of the following is not great, and most are off page, the sensitive topics may be unsettling for some readers.

Triggers include: Anxiety, Body Shaming (Disfigurmisia), Disordered Weight & Body Thoughts, Fear, Off-Page Depression, Off-Page Gaslighting, Off-Page Previous Mentally and Emotionally Abusive Relationship with Abandonment, Off-Page Pressure to Maintain a Certain Image, Undiagnosed Post Traumatic Stress Disorder, Mention of the word "torture" but used in the way to describe a feeling, Mention of men being controlling, Mention of Infringement of Personal Space.

Please be sure to provide self-care above all else.

Love always,

Loren Sorensen

the *Trouble* with *Christmas* playlist

There's No Way (Feat. Julia Michaels) | Lauv
September | James Arthur
Issues | Julia Michaels
Heart Out | The 1975
Lavendar Haze | Taylor Swift
3 Libras | A Perfect Circle
If You Need Me | Julia Michaels
Sucker | The Jonas Brothers
Fallingforyou | the 1975
Check Yes, Juliet | We the Kings
Everlong—Acoustic Version | The Foo Fighters
Worst of Me | Julia Michaels
As It Was | Harry Styles
I Wanna Be Yours | Arctic Monkeys
Robbers | The 1975
Stolen | Dashboard Confessional
Little Did I Know | Julia Michaels
It Was Always You | Maroon 5
Hands Down—Dashboard Confessional

listen on spotify and apple music

spotify   apple music

Rayanne's christmas playlist

It's Beginning to Look a Lot like Christmas | Michael Bublé
Carol of the Bells | John Williams
Merry Christmas Baby | Hanson
Merry Christmas, Happy Holidays | *NSYNC
All I Want for Christmas Is You | Mariah Carey
What Christmas Means To Me | Hanson
Making Christmas (from 'The Nightmare Before Christmas') | Penatonix
Santa Baby | Eartha Kitt
Holly Jolly Christmas | Michael Bublé
Let it Snow! Let it Snow! Let it Snow! | Frank Sinatra
Jingle Bell Rock | Bobby Helms
Last Christmas | Wham!
Christmas (Please Come Home) | Hanson
Santa Tell Me | Ariana Grande
White Christmas | Otis Redding
O Holy Night - A Capella | *NSYNC
Have Yourself A Merry Little Christmas | Christina Aguilera
Winter Wonderland | Eurythmics
Do You Hear What I Hear? | Whitney Houston
The Christmas Song (Chestnuts Roasting on an Open Fire) | *NSYNC
Christmas Time is Here | Vince Guaraldi Trio

listen on spotify and apple music

spotify   apple music

rayanne

THERE'S NO WAY (FEAT. JULIA
MICHAELS) | LAUV

'Tis the season, and I *still* don't have my Christmas tree.

With ten days to go until Christmas, I've been unsuccessful in my attempts to check off that one box on my to-do list. Is it because my family's already traveling out of town for the season? They're on their holidays and my best friend, Isla, is set to leave for an extended holiday in England with that smoking hot boyfriend of hers. Unfortunately, she's too busy working out of town until she leaves.

Had Isla been here, we would have sorted out how to manage the tree together, first by dragging it up the three flights of stairs of my apartment building, laughing our way up each turn that led us to my apartment. And somehow, after we managed to recover from that, we'd create some sort of pulley system for getting the tree standing upright. It would have been a pain in our asses, but at least we would have entertained each other the whole time.

I chuckle at the thought. I'm definitely in over my head trying to do this all by myself. Between picking my Christmas tree, getting it to my apartment, and stabilizing it in my tree stand, I have a lot to do to complete the perfect Christmas vision. While I'd love nothing more than to have my bestie here with me, I can't begrudge Isla her happiness. She deserves it and that sweet Englishman of hers.

Too bad he only has sisters.

Moving into my new apartment this year was an unexpected highlight. The first thing I saw when the door opened were ten-foot ceilings and a vast window overlooking Austin's skyline. My vision tunneled and all I saw was my future flashing before my eyes: me, in this apartment with a gorgeous Christmas tree centered in front of the city's stunning skyline. I said yes to the real estate agent instantly.

Standing for the first time in a while, I arch my body into a back bending stretch, then walk over to my linen closet to determine where I can find my Christmas tree stand easily. Towels and other important linens are stuffed in front of it, and a giggle bursts from me involuntarily when I find it. It doesn't matter, and it shouldn't be that exciting, but I couldn't afford the tree of my dreams last year. I was stuck with a standard six-foot tree, and this is the only base I have.

A Christmas tree stand is six of one, half a dozen of the other. I can't imagine that it'll make that much of a difference for whatever beauty I find this year.

This shouldn't be a big deal, right?

I walk back to my living room and place my tree stand

where I want it, then run to the furthest opposite corner to inspect the overall effect. I cackle with delight, jumping up and down, as it officially looks like Christmas vomited all over my apartment. Fairy lights trace the window frame with melting snow decals which lay smooth against my huge bay windows. I spent ages making this vision come to life. Garlands are placed on the mantles and cover the door jambs of my front entrance. All that's needed now is the tree.

Our family's always favored Fraser trees growing up. Christmas has always been a family affair; with my mother's Scandinavian background and my father's southern roots, it was inevitable that my apartment would look like a Christmas advertisement in a magazine. All that's left is that perfect Fraser fir decorated top to bottom with twinkling lights at night.

Frasers are in high demand in Austin unfortunately, and it seems like everyone else shares my vision. Thankfully there are enough still in town. I know, because I checked with a couple of tree farms in the greater Austin area. I just need to figure out how to get the tree to my apartment, up three stories of stairs, then make it stand correctly to become the magnificent centerpiece it was always meant to be.

There's an answer to my dilemma, but I'm not ready to call in the favor just yet. Caleb, a twenty-five-year-old who has muscles for days, could easily help me lift my tree up three flights of stairs and position it into the tree holder. The only problem is that he is Isla's younger brother who's been making doe eyes at me since he was thirteen. We haven't addressed this crush, which is fine by me. It was awkward ten years ago when we saw each other regularly, but we don't see each other enough to make me feel self-conscious about it anymore.

You'd think your best friend would recognize the dilemma and help dissolve any awkward tension, but Isla clearly thrives in the tension. She teases me anytime Caleb's name comes up, and I have to pretend I don't know what she's talking about. Her wide, mischievous grin settles in my mind. Between the two Gardiner siblings, it often feels crowded in my head.

With all my hard work completed, I decide to reward myself with a cup of tea and walk into my kitchen to start up my electric kettle. Isla's love for tea bled into my own life and I start my ritual with lining my cup with sugar so that it's the perfect amount of sweet and prepare my tea bag for water.

I watch the bubbles grow in the tea kettle as the water heats. I'm not sure exactly how I'm going to get my Christmas tree up to my apartment. My brows furrow in concern as I try to figure out logistics that don't involve Caleb. He is, unfortunately, the only person I know to ask right now for help.

I just… I just don't want to be put in a position where he gets his hopes up because we're joking around, and we become so comfortable around one another that he accidentally interprets it as romantic interest. We've always been so easy around each other, and I don't want to risk flipping a switch on that I have no interest in pursuing. I don't want to hurt him.

I haven't had to deal with Caleb's puppy eyes on a regular basis since he went to culinary school and got his master's degree as a pastry chef four years ago. He was recruited for the Head Pastry Chef position at *Les Portes du Plaisir* in the final semester of his degree. Since I left for college, we've lived separate lives, and I've essentially lost contact with him as an adult. The only times we really see each other now are when Isla is in town.

I sigh, acknowledging that had Caleb not been Isla's brother, I might reconsider those puppy dog eyes begging me for attention. They're a soulful rich brown that matches his chestnut hair.

And granted, his hair almost achieves sex-hair status, with the perfect amount of curve falling into his eyes. His body is sculpted with precision from mixing ingredients all day and who knows what else. And... damnit! Caleb is actually the perfect height for jumping into arms that I know would catch me...

But he is Isla's kid brother and we've just known each other too long.

To ever consider Caleb as anything more is just... weird.

The tea kettle beeps its notification that my water is ready, so I pour it into my teacup and let it brew. When it's steeped to my preferred strength, I pour a dash of milk into my cup. I make my way back to my couch and settle in. The warmth of the mug rests comfortably as I hold it close to my chest and inhale the fragrant scent of the tea while taking my first sip.

The memories catch me by the dozens as I drink my tea slowly. I remember when Caleb was about six or seven, sneaking around the corner of the kitchen trying to catch Isla and me in our late-night rendezvous with our beloved cookie dough. How many bargains did we make with him so he would leave us alone?

And then... somewhere between our junior and senior year in high school, Caleb started baking on a serious level and Isla and I found ourselves in a situation where we had to negotiate for our cookie dough for our inadvisable consumption. I'm deeply suspicious that he made too much because Caleb knew how much eating raw cookie dough was too integral to our regular hangout routine.

I involuntarily smile at the memories, which sour into a frown as I double back on the fact that I consider Caleb to be attractive. Could I imagine something more with him?

God, no! It's truly inconceivable. He is three years

younger than me, and I can envision the child, the awkward teenager, and the budding hottie all in one reel of moving pictures. It's so hard to not associate the kid I met first, especially since we grew up together. We were the last two standing when shit hit the fan. We found ourselves reaching for each other when Isla lost her baby and their father abandoned their family. Caleb came to me for comfort and guidance, and the barrier that separated us was forgotten.

He's important to me, and we've impacted each other all our lives. And… it's precisely for this reason that considering Caleb anything other than Isla's brother is unacceptable.

But does that really mean he can't help me find a Christmas tree?

God, this logic sucks.

Fine. He's perfect for the job.

And *fine*: these days, when I see Caleb around Isla's apartment, there might be a fan girl swooning at those arms and that damned cheeky grin, daring me.

And *fine*: I'm scared shitless of being alone with him because we have shared our past histories.

But I can hang out with Caleb on my own.

No Isla necessary.

If it means that I can get my perfect tree in the apartment, then I'll just have to work hard to make sure there are no distractions or unnecessary temptations. I've gone twelve years without breaking his heart and maintaining a solid distance. I can go another weekend without anything else happening.

Right?

caleb

SEPTEMBER | JAMES ARTHUR

It's ten o'clock in the evening, and I'm biding my time as I wait for Celeste—or Chelsea, whatever her name is —to fall asleep. When she's sound asleep, I'll slip out of her bed discretely and shoot her a text. Something meaningful about our time together, but nothing too personal. We'll text for a couple of days, and perhaps another time if I decide to sleep with her again. Girls these days usually aren't looking for post it notes on the refrigerator or on the kitchen island like movies would lead you to believe. A text works, so that's what they get.

I'm not really interested in pursuing second dates with

women most days, so I've become a master at letting them tell me when they don't feel that spark anymore. It works out, because it's usually what I want.

Am I a coward or a bastard for taking this route? My friends constantly rib into me with their endless opinions, but the truth is that it's easy. I don't lie to these girls, but I don't make a point of overly sharing my feelings either. One girl told me I had the "mysterious attractive best friend" vibes, and I honestly have no idea what it means. But she was dumping me at a convenient time, so I didn't take it personally.

Honestly?

I forgot to care after she said it.

My phone from under the pillow buzzes. I wrap my fingers around it and look at it quizzically. My friends know the deal, know my routine, and that I'm trying to make a smooth exit out the door now. I'll usually get a text around midnight just to make sure I got home safely. Then they all have a laugh at me in the morning when I tell them about my "walks of shame" back to my apartment. But there is no shame, and it's all been a good time. After all, that's the point of surrounding myself with beautiful women. Isn't it?

I pull my phone out from my pillow discretely and focus on the notification. My eyes must not have seen clearly, because it's Rayanne Miller texting me.

Jesus.

Rayanne Miller.

My sister's best friend, and the only girl I'd never walk away from, should I ever experience spending more than a few moments alone with her. Her heart-shaped face is framed in insatiable curls that make her hair the embodiment of temptation. I've been dying to dig my fingers into it since I knew what a hard on was. Rayanne was the first girl of my wet dreams, and the only girl I'd ever offer my heart to—if she asked.

Too bad that's never going to happen. Four years ago, I began making a valiant effort to kick her out of my mind and heart. It helps that we don't cross paths unless Isla is in town and we're in forced social circumstances.

Rayanne's beauty punches me in the gut every time I see her, but it's her candid skepticism and humor, and the way she makes my sister laugh like she's never felt pain that captivates my imagination. It's the way Rayanne bursts with laughter when I say something entertaining that she doesn't expect. It's that small smile on her face she tries to hide when she remembers how long we've known one another. It's the way we know how to comfort each other when our trauma hits us unexpectedly, or we're left to our own devices.

The attempts to forget Rayanne Miller for the last four years evaporate with the text notification. My mind is already spiraling out of control the minute I hear from Rayanne. I'm ready to do her bidding—should she ever bid me to do anything. And I haven't even read the damn text message yet.

I hit my head on the pillow—then look immediately to my left to make sure I didn't bother Celeste.

Celeste?

I shake my head, redoubling my efforts to focus my concentration.

God, this always happens. I thought I had better control this time, which of course I don't. When it comes to Rayanne, I'm not sure I'll ever command my emotions. I've been too deep into these feelings for too long now, whether I like it or not.

I have my moments of being a real asshole at times, but even I understand it's best not to read Rayanne's text in Chelsea's bed. I sit up carefully so I don't disturb her. I discretely glide out carefully of the bed and glance back at her.

Yeah, she's totally a Chelsea. I don't know why I ever thought her name was Celeste.

Dressing quickly, I step into the hallway with my possessions in my pockets or hands. I text Chelsea something self-deprecating about my work schedule, knowing it'll pull on the corners of her mouth until she's smiling instead of frowning at my disappearance.

Being mindful of Chelsea, I walk back to my truck and tap my phone once more to see that Rayanne is texting again. I tap on my phone to discover what her deal is.

RAY MILLER

Hey Caleb.

'Tis the season and I'm late picking a Christmas tree. Again.

Any chance you can help me out with this?

This is about a Christmas tree!?
Of course, it is.

The Millers are a cut above the rest in their Christmas game as they vomit the holiday season everywhere they go.

A sigh involuntarily escapes as I open my phone up to read the rest of her text message.

RAY MILLER

I don't want to inconvenience you, it's just that everyone else is out of town, and I need you.

Send help?

I scoff at the idea of Rayanne inconveniencing me at all. Of course, I'm a last resort. That damn crush of mine has always held her at arm's length from me. If I had known how

18

to keep my cool around her when I was younger, perhaps I wouldn't be the last person she'd ask for help. I type out a response just to get it over with, then step up into my truck and turn the engine on.

CALEB GARDINER

Yeah, I'll be there.

Just tell me when and where.

My head meets the steering wheel the minute I see the message is delivered and groan aloud. Of course I'm going to help Rayanne. It's just that every time we come across each other, I'm perpetually caught between teenager Caleb and the man I've grown into today. One minute I'm making her laugh, and the next she's looking up at me through her lashes and I've transformed back to that awkward thirteen-year-old who just discovered exactly how girls transform into goddesses.

Of course, I'll help her.

But someone do me a solid and just help me get my ass together, so I don't act like a fucking idiot the whole time we are getting her tree into her apartment.

caleb

HEART OUT | THE 1975

I barely have a moment to tap on Rayanne's door because she opens it with a wide, generous smile almost immediately as I arrive. Her long blonde curls bounce with greeting as her baby blue eyes shine with eagerness. I know Rayanne's enthusiasm exists only because I'm helping her with her Christmas tree, but it's been a hot minute since I've seen her. My breath catches in my throat, captivated by how beautiful she is. In the month since I last saw her at Isla's, I've managed to forget how much she affects me. It's like this *Every. Damn. Time.* Anything I was going to say is lost as I look at Rayanne for the first time in weeks.

Christmas garlands and twinkling lights greet me from the living room. She has done everything she possibly can to decorate her apartment, and I'll admit, Rayanne has done a great job. I look down at her and smile.

"Hi!" Rayanne greets me. "Like what you see?"

I like everything I see about you.

"Hey," I reply. Thank god I sound normal because I feel my heart racing like I'm a teenager again. My smile widens as I scan what she's wearing. Her outfit is completely ridiculous, beginning with an oversized Christmas tree sweater, skinny jeans, and combat boots. Of course, she's wearing a Christmas sweater on a sixty-degree December morning. Her jeans hug her in all the right places, but the sweater hides all those gorgeous curves. And those combat boots…

Fuck. They get me every time. Only Rayanne would put together an outfit like this and not give two shits about how an oversized Christmas sweater looks with combat boots.

"Nice outfit." I chuckle, tugging on the tails of her sweater.

"Thanks," Rayanne beams at me, bouncing on the toes of her boots. She's completely unaware of me checking her out. "You ready?"

"Yeah." I can't help it. I tug on her curls, and she swats at me, laughing.

"Come on, let's go!" Rayanne pokes my arm. "The Christmas tree farm is in Cedar Park and we got half an hour of traffic ahead of us."

"Of course you're dragging me that far up north to Cedar Park...for a Christmas tree," I complain, rolling my eyes. We're going to have to drive on a national highway, full of potential traffic jams, or possible accidents with a Christmas tree.

This is going to be a *disaster.*

"Well, *duh,*" Rayanne pokes my side rather insistently,

again. "Get going, Gardiner. My perfect Christmas tree won't be there forever. It's waiting for me."

"You do know that this is heavy work, right?" I ask, tugging on her sweater again. "You might reconsider?" I quirk a questioning brow in her direction.

"Pfft," Rayanne dismisses the notion. "This sweater's going to be good luck. Come on, Caleb."

"You're going to be pulling it off in two hours," I warn. "It's nice outside, but it's too warm for this thing."

"I'll be fine," Rayanne insists.

"Don't get mad if I tell you I told you so later," I smirk.

Rayanne rolls her eyes and tugs on my hand, urging me forward. "Come on," She nudges me out of her doorway. "My Christmas tree is waiting."

"Right," I reply, exhaling. "You keep talking about your Christmas tree like it's a puppy dog waiting to get adopted."

Rayanne snorts as commentary, "Try to keep up, Caleb." She steps around me to start climbing down the stairs.

I sigh, knowing this is going to be a long ass day. Getting involved with Rayanne Miller and her Christmas tree is trouble. I know how her parents made Christmas come alive during the season and how that affected her expectations. She'll be chasing memories of her childhood in an apartment that is too small for her grand vision. While a Christmas tree will make it complete, I know she's expecting something majestic. She wants this tree *big*. But we don't need something like a nine-footer to experience the magic she's trying to create.

At that thought I cringe internally... God, we're going to have to get whatever she picks up these stairs into her apartment.

"You had to pick an apartment on the third story, didn't you?" I complain once more, keeping pace beside her. "These

23

stairs are going to be pains in our asses dragging whatever tree you pick up to your apartment."

"Yeah, Caleb," Rayanne offers me a gorgeous smile, pulling on all my heart strings. "That's why I have you."

You have no idea, Rayanne Lee Miller.

I exhale slowly, indulging for a moment, imagining what it would look like if she would let me sweep her off her feet. The thought of caging Rayanne in and pressing her against a wall as I kiss her senseless is a sight that leaves me breathless. I imagine ripping that ridiculous sweater off Rayanne's body, just so I could show her how much I appreciate all those beautiful curves. I groan aloud when I realize that I've stopped walking. Today is not starting off well.

Rayanne actually *skips* over to my truck, waiting for me to beep it open. I grin helplessly at her as I unlock the doors and watch her yank the door open. The hinges protest at her enthusiasm. She takes a deep breath and hops into my truck. I chuckle, listening to her *oomph* as she lands in the passenger seat. The truck adjusts to her weight, and I start the ignition for the truck knowing she's safely seated inside. I open the back seat door behind the driver's side, rummaging for a fresh undershirt. Rayanne's mission for finding a Christmas tree is going to be physically demanding, so I change into a new one, anticipating the hard, sweaty work climbing up that apartment stairwell.

"Ready?" I ask, climbing into the driver's side.

"Caleb, I've been ready since—" Rayanne moves her legs up and down like a little kid who has ants in her pants.

"Stupid question," I grin, looking down at her. "Let's go."

The drive to the tree farm doesn't take too long, but I do notice enough traffic that's cluttering into traffic jams going south. There are a few cars heading back to their homes with trees stuck on the tops. I'm grateful that I have a truck because the tree will be safe in the bed. The end of the trunk might stick out of my truck, which I'm only mindful of because people are assholes when they drive on I-35. Should the tree get damaged, Rayanne's going to cut somebody's head off. For the sake of everyone's safety, it's best we get this tree to her apartment in one piece.

As soon as the ignition turns off, Rayanne bursts from the truck like a shooting star and I'm barely able to keep her in my line of vision. I know exactly what she's looking for, and it's not appropriate to what the apartment can handle.

"Rayanne," I yell after her. "Don't you dare pick a nine-footer!"

"Of course, I'm picking a nine-footer," she turns around, flashing me a grin as she walks backwards. She looks positively radiant, like a little kid in a candy store. "I finally have an apartment that lets me have a big tree!"

"Fuck," I mutter. This is a problem. "Don't you dare!" I yell at her, but it's to Rayanne's back, and she's positively ignoring me. I blink once, and she's disappeared into the maze of Christmas trees. I sigh as I shrug my shoulders and hook my thumbs through the belt loop of my jeans. Blonde curls flash in front of me, and I start moving towards the back, where the flash of Rayanne's hair gave her away.

"OH. My. God!" Rayanne's voice shouts out a few minutes later. It's loud and filled with excitement and anticipation. "*Ohmigod, Caleb*! I found it!"

"Aw, fuck," I mutter.

Here we go.

Let's test out how far back she went. "Where are you?"

"Back here!" she replies. It's far enough that I have to quicken my pace. The longer that I am separated from her, the more set Rayanne will become on whatever tree she's chosen. And then it'll be a fucking nightmare for me to pick up the pieces.

"*Marco!*" I shout. We've played this game with Isla since

25

we knew we could play outside by ourselves but it's now just a joke between the three of us. There was a time during our school years where Isla included me in everything she did with Rayanne. It's a testament to her being the best fucking sister there is in the world because she didn't leave me hanging.

"*Polo!*" Rayanne shouts, then giggles delightfully. I grin helplessly when I find her. She's a fucking beacon of light. With laughter dancing in her eyes, she makes a big *TADA* gesture at the tree with her whole body, arms extended out with jazz hands dancing, with her legs supporting her new position.

Aw, fuck me. I'm going to have to talk her down from this, just like I knew I would. The tree, as she predictably told me, is a nine-and-a-half-foot Fraser. According to Isla, the Millers insist that the whole point of a Christmas tree is to have a shining star on the top. If that's the case, this tree is going to barely stand without scraping the top of the ceiling. The needles fan out beautifully, but the width of the bottom of the tree will spread too wide and it will take up all the free walking space in her living room. Then there's also the fact that this tree looks sturdy enough to knock me down on my ass and could send me tumbling down three flights of stairs if I miss a step or stumble.

Not worth it.

"No," I say, crossing my arms.

"No?" Rayanne replies, raising an eyebrow. "Why ever *not?*" The final T in "not" is enunciated crisply to pronounce her disfavor.

Sorry, your Highness, we're fighting this out.

"Where do I begin?" I scoff with laughter.

"From the beginning." Rayanne crosses her own arms, and the battle of reason and logic versus nostalgia and vision has commenced.

"The tree's too fucking tall, Rayanne," I begin at the top of my list. "You won't be able to light up a star at the top."

"I'll use a bow," she rallies defensively.

"Ray," I roll my eyes. "When the fuck have you ever decorated with a bow?"

"I can trim the top!" Her deflection is a point to me because Rayanne Miller has never used a fucking bow for decorating in her life.

"Then it's going to look disproportionate, and the top will look too full and short." I argue, knowing how much it matters to Rayanne. "And you won't be satisfied with inadequate proportions."

"Who cares?" Rayanne fires back, her arms flying up in frustration.

"You will!"

"The tree is freaking gorgeous," Rayanne counters, stomping her foot. "It'll look perfect in my apartment."

"And how do you propose getting this thing up there?" I raise my own eyebrow. "Unless you're willing to pay the farm for a pulley and are prepared to contest noise complaints with the apartment complex because we'll be trying to get this damn thing up there. *We* are not enough."

"I have a dolley," she rejoins defensively. "And you brought your straps."

"Fine," I retort, my arms flying up with frustration. "Where will your furniture go? This damn tree is too big in your living room. You won't even be able to walk through it, let alone sit and relax to enjoy it without the tree suffocating you."

"Damnit, Caleb!" Rayanne's eyes widen with emotion, and she's about to go full temper tantrum on me. Honestly, I don't know how Isla puts up with this shit because Rayanne is so fucking stubborn. "It's perfect," she whispers. "It's everything I've envisioned this whole year. Just… let me have this."

Something in her tone makes me relent. It wasn't that long ago I remember she wasn't always allowed to make all her own choices for herself. That ex of hers was a nasty piece of work, and for the sake of that woman from a few years ago, I let it go.

I huff, walk towards the tree, and look at the price, which is fucking outrageous. "Seriously?"

"I can afford it," she states, eyes turning to blue steel.

Fucking hell, she's still fighting. The impulse to fight back is biting, but I let it go against my better judgment. "It's a fucking scam." I reply, snorting with disgust.

"God, you and Isla can be such assholes, you know that?" Rayanne huffs. I smirk internally because if either of us looked into a mirror, we'd be the perfect reflection of each other's expressions. Arms crossed at our chests, an individual eyebrow raised and a look of pure stubborn contempt for the other's logic.

"Yeah, guess it runs in the family," I mutter, the words tasting bitter in my mouth. The ghost of my father and the abandonment of our family settle in the shadows between us. The lingering effects are transparent as Rayanne's eyes widen. I didn't mean to bring up Arnold, but I know she's interpreted my comment with him in mind.

"Oh, Caleb—" she softens, and that tender look in her eyes is a kick to my balls.

"It's whatever." I scuff my boots against the ground, conceding. "Get the fucking tree, Rayanne. It makes you happy." I walk back to the truck to grant myself some space. I'll just make sure the truck is ready to go for loading when the Christmas tree is ready.

Rayanne knows all the secrets and skeletons that lay hidden in my closet, and her reaction to the mention of my father only reminds me of what stands bare between us. For the most part, my life has been blessed, but my trauma resides solely in my father's dissatisfaction with our family. It started with his gaslighting and attempt to blame us for his unhappiness and led to his eventual abandonment of us when I was fifteen. That doesn't include what lies between him and Isla. And when Isla wasn't there to offer me comfort, Rayanne was there for all of it. When Dad left, it was her touch I sought for comfort, and she offered it willingly. When it got worse, and our trauma kicked us around more, it was Rayanne's fortifying hugs that settled me and became my beacon of strength. I wouldn't be who I am today without her.

Arms wrap around me from behind and hug my waist. Rayanne mumbles into the dip between my shoulder blades. "I didn't mean to be a dick."

"Yeah, I know." I sigh and turn around to hug her properly. Her honey almond scent is intoxicating. My fingers brush her hair out of her face. The feeling of our skin flush against each other is the gentlest of grazes, but it's a match set to flames. Touching Rayanne fuels my demand for her, and I didn't know how much I've needed it until now. I resist holding her tighter against me because this is an embrace of friendship, nothing more. This is Rayanne, my sister's best friend, not my consolation prize for rewarding me with strength.

I sigh, resigned. "Sorry for being a dick too, but I stand by what I said," I murmur against her temple. "That tree is going to be a fucking nightmare."

"Right," she replies, and I feel her smile grow on my chest. I feel like Hercules when Zeus turned him into a god when she releases the embrace. "I'll eat my words, I'm sure."

"You will," I reply, my own smile turning at the corners of my mouth. "And I'll be the first one to make sure you know it." I'll shamelessly rub it in her face when I'm proven right. The thing about Rayanne is that she'll take it with grace and laugh with me. It's always been like this between us.

"Fine," she huffs. "I need to go pay and show them where the truck is."

"I'll take care of the tree." I reply. "Just take care of the payment and we'll get out of here."

I head back to the tree and find it's already been taken out of its stand. One of the staff members has laid it down horizontally, trimming the trunk for its own nourishment as it arrives at Rayanne's apartment. I start inspecting the quality of the tree on Rayanne's behalf, knowing exactly what she wants. The top could get trimmed down a few inches which might give us enough space for her to put up a star.

"Hey man, any chance we can trim this a few inches down?" I say to the guy with the hand saw. "Rayanne's going to want to put a star on this tree and it's barely going to fit in her apartment as it is."

He grins at me, "Sure, no problem."

As he follows my request, I turn my head to assess how full the tree will be at the top. I find a few other places that might help shape the tree a little more to accommodate her apartment and point them out. "And is it okay if we get these trimmed down a bit too?"

"Did your girlfriend ask you to do this?" he asks, like he hears these sorts of requests all the time.

"Nah, man." I shake my head. "She didn't ask, and she's just a family friend." He pauses from his work and turns to look at me.

"She's not your girlfriend?"

"Nope," I reiterate. "We've just known each other forever."

He shakes his head in disbelief, and I raise a brow at his reaction. He takes to his work, trimming down the places I've requested. When he's done, he purses his lips as if he has something else to say.

"What?" I ask, unable to resist the bait.

"Well, it's just that she *should* be your girlfriend," he says, a knowing grin spreading. "It's none of my business, I know, but we all saw your shouting match about the tree. And those were the fighting words of a couple, my friend."

At my look of astonishment, he chuckles. "Look, I'm sorry, but I've got a loud mouth with endless opinions. And someone had to say it." He looks slightly sheepish at the admission, but not enough to be truly apologetic.

I offer him a small smile, conceding his point. "Regardless of what *should* happen," I sigh with frustration, annoyed that a stranger can see our connection and Rayanne is completely clueless. "I don't think Rayanne's changing her mind anytime soon."

"Would you mind helping me lift this to your car?" the tree guy asks, seemingly changing the subject. "All the other associates are helping customers. I'm Chris, by the way."

"Caleb," I reply and shake his proffered hand. "And sure, no problem."

We count together and heave the tree onto our shoulders, then find a steady pace to the truck with me leading the way. We arrive at the truck and lower it steadily on the bed so that the heavy end of the tree is supported in the bed with the last few feet sticking out. It looks secure, but who knows what stupid things could happen on our drive back into Austin. Making quick work of an easy job, Chris and I are left to our own devices. When we're done, we lean against the truck, observing the tree farm, its customers, and the kids running around, playing hide and seek.

"Do you *want* her to be your girlfriend?" he asks, pointedly.

It's been almost ten minutes since he brought Rayanne up. I thought we were done with this conversation.

Fuck me, this guy is like a dog with a bone, unable to drop the topic.

"It doesn't matter what I want." I retort, dragging the words out. These are truths I don't care to discuss at the moment. The guy can't take a fucking hint.

"That's a yes then," Chris raises a brow at me, looking right through my reluctance.

"Fine, it's a yes." I sigh, dragging the truth out reluctantly. Chris is stripping away at facts that I don't usually talk about. My friends have no idea, and Isla may be the only person suspicious of how deep my feelings run for Rayanne. But we haven't discussed the facts of my heart or how vast my affection extends for her. I want Rayanne to be mine, ever since I grasped the notion of what it means to be a boyfriend to someone. I *want* to be hers.

"What gives, man?" I finally cave, asking the question that's been bursting to escape. "Why the interest in my love life?"

"I told you, I'm a nosy bastard and I like sharing unnecessary opinions." He snort laughs, and shrugs like it's no big deal. "But it also turns out that I won over my lady finally, and you two remind me of where we were a year ago."

"Congrats, man." I offer a tentative smile. The warmth of the sun shining down reminds me that I need to stay hydrated and I turn to the back of my truck to grab water bottles. "Hey, you want some water?" I really don't need to invite further conversation, but I do it anyway.

"If you have one to spare, that'd be great." I open the truck door and grab two water bottles and hand one to him. "Thanks for this," Chris says, and twists the top off to take a swig.

After a moment he asks, "Have you tried talking to her?"

"No," I shrug helplessly. "I don't think she's interested in me that way."

"Oh, she's into you," he snorts. "She just doesn't know it yet."

"How do you know?" I reply, leaning back against the truck bed and turning my gaze to the sun, seeking its comforting warmth.

"Something about the familiarity between you two," Chris says. "And the way you fought. Y'all got chemistry, that's for sure."

"We've been fighting since we were kids," I scoff dismissively. "Ray's my sister's best friend and we basically grew up together." Chris grins his appreciation.

"And look, I appreciate the vote of confidence about her interest." I continue on a sigh, "But she's never given me an ounce of encouragement to pursue anything with her." It still hurts, even after all this time. I dig the toe of my boot into the ground to release some of my frustration.

"How much do y'all know each other now?" he asks. At my puzzled look, he continues, "Like, when was the last time y'all hung out? Was it ever just the two of you?"

"No," I concede. "We basically only see each other when my sister is in town."

"Caleb, man, she doesn't know who you are now," Chris brightens as he sees possibility. "You need to help her out. Spend some time together so you can nudge her in the right direction. It can't hurt, right?"

"And how do you suggest I do that?" I ask, giving up any pride I have. Honestly, it's nice having someone to sort out these feelings and the issues that come with them. Chris is separated enough from the situation that if he perhaps sees hope for us, then maybe I can too.

"Well, y'all are hauling this tree into her apartment, right?" he asks.

"Yes," I reply with a groan, not looking forward to it.

"There's plenty of opportunity there," he says, tapping knowingly on his temple.

"Yeah, I'm not sure there is," I reply, laughing. All I can see is trying to navigate this impending disaster of an errand.

"Open your eyes, man," he counters. "You'll figure it out. Lots of opportunities for falling on your asses and brushing needles out of each other's hair. You don't know what the possibilities are, especially if you don't try." He winks at me knowingly, and I scoff. Before I can comment, Rayanne comes within hearing distance, putting an abrupt end to the conversation.

"Thanks for all your help today!" Rayanne offers her hand to Chris.

"No problem, miss," he says. "Enjoy your tree, and Merry Christmas." Chris offers me his hand to shake with that knowing look that says I'm allowed hope if that's what I want. He's suggesting the promise of change just by simply lining up the dominoes. If she tells me no, then I know my answer for good and I've done all I can. After all, avoiding these constant deep feelings has never worked. If I risk it all, at least I know my answer for good.

"It was good talking," I finally reply, offering him a small smile as we shake hands. "Merry Christmas, and thanks for the help."

"Anytime," he says. "Merry Christmas."

rayanne

3 LIBRAS | A PERFECT CIRCLE |
SUCKER | JONAS BROTHERS

I should be furious with Caleb. I really want to be. He's gone and pissed me off by listing all the ways my perfect tree is wrong for my apartment. But then the *asshole* comment happened, and I instantly felt like the dick in this situation. He didn't mean to bring up his dad, and I certainly didn't mean to. It's just that Arnold really did a number on Caleb growing up and I'm never going to stop being sorry for what happened to their family. I can't help it if I feel protective of Caleb. I've seen what it looks like when he's hurt, and I just want to make it better... if I can.

Don't get me wrong; Caleb is still the prize winner for the

biggest dick at the tree farm award. But I know what his family has gone through and know how good of a man Rebecca raised him to be. And yes, his usual MO runs with a bad temper, a Class A Jerk most days. He's nosy, constantly over-sharing unwanted opinions, and a pain in Isla's and my ass. But he's *our* pain in the ass.

Caleb's quiet in the truck on the drive back to my apartment. I'm not sure what to do with myself, because I can't really tell if he's just pissy with me for picking the perfect tree, or if something else is on his mind. I don't know if I want to start small talk or if I want to ask more probing questions. Outside of our past history and whatever Isla volunteers, I honestly don't know much about him. Isla has always been a buffer between the two of us. And without her here, the current silence between us is the weird and awkward kind.

Traffic is at a standstill. I tap my feet restlessly against the glove compartment of his trunk, trying to figure out what to do next. I scroll through my music, just to find something—any and all inspiration will do. We need to find that good vibe we always have. I know we've been to a couple of concerts together, so that might start us on track again. Caleb and I have been to a couple of concerts together, but always in the company of a large group of friends. Still, I know that we share some common music interests—Isla's said so, but I don't know exactly where to start.

"Here," Caleb says, breaking the silence. He tosses me his phone open for perusal. I smile at him gratefully because his Bluetooth is connected to his truck and we can immediately start our jam session.

"Where do you prefer to listen to music these days?" I ask, wondering if I should look for an app, Apple Music, or something else.

Caleb shrugs. "Spotify, but pick your poison. We still

have—" he checks his watch then glances out into traffic, "Forty minutes to go before we hit your exit."

"Stupid Austin traffic." I grumble, and Caleb chuckles at me.

I open up Spotify and navigate to his liked songs. Caleb has a wide and eclectic taste, which I bet he has Isla to thank for. I see a bit of ska, lots of punk, some metal. A lot of the music has a nostalgic touch to it. I grin helplessly as I see a lot of Panic! At the Disco, Dashboard Confessional, Fall Out Boy, and The 1975.

"Good stuff, Caleb." I grin at him. "I'm impressed."

"Those are my go-to these days," he comments, shrugging. "Though I've just discovered A Perfect Circle after going through a Tool phase a few months ago. They're currently on repeat."

"Maynard Keenan is a freaking genius," I reply, searching for *3 Libras*. When I find it, I tap to begin the song. The violins begin, soothing my soul and my heart soars with the movement of the orchestra. As Maynard moves through the verses of the song, I find myself dying with happiness just a little bit.

"Aww man." Caleb grins back at me. "I freaking love this song."

"Absolutely," I agree. "The progression at the end is amazing. I feel like crying every time I hear it." I sing the ending to make my point. I feel the release of the music revitalizing my soul.

"How does that go again?" Caleb teases, laughing at me.

"Shut up," I laugh, thwacking him on his arm.

"Heeeey! No hitting the driver while in motion!" Caleb tsks me.

"Sorry! Sorry!" I surrender, arms up.

The second verse starts, and we both follow Maynard's words. Caleb has the voice of an angel as he follows all of

Maynard's cadences and passion. This song is heartbreaking, dynamic, and gorgeous. As we lead into the chorus, we're both singing at the top of our lungs, Caleb plays air violin and at the buildup to the end, we're both playing air drums and singing so loud that the bass vibrates the car. The song ends abruptly, and I quirk my lips down, disappointed. I instantly put it on repeat, and Caleb grins at me.

"So, hey, we make a good team." he says, a smile quirking on the corner of his lips. My cheeks turn pink at the notion of us being anything together. "Nice call on the repeat."

"It's generally the appropriate reaction to hearing the end of that song." I shrug, a small grin turning up on my lips. "At least it's mine." I turn back Caleb's phone to resume scrolling through his music. I search for a new song to sing together— less dynamically, of course, because traffic is finally moving. I let *3 Libras* end properly the playlist shuffles automatically to *Sucker* by the Jonas Brothers.

"Really?" I raise an eyebrow at him, trying to hide my smile.

While the Jonas Brothers are not what I call my normal jam, Isla turned me on to their newer music. It's so fucking catchy that it's hard not to move to the beat. When they came to Austin a few years ago, Isla bought tickets and made me go with her and some friends. I was surprised to find most of the audience were my age. To my complete shock, the concert was a fucking blast and we had an amazing time.

"Their riffs are catchy!" Caleb laughs. "You do remember I went to the concert with y'all, right?"

"That's right!" I yell in excitement, smacking his arm. "God, that was a good concert."

"Yeah, it was." Caleb replies, then completely astonishes me as he hits Nick's falsetto perfectly as he leads into the chorus. The guy is a regular Sinatra, and I'm completely impressed. I sing the backup, and Caleb starts whistling.

"Oh my God, stop!" I start laughing. "When did you become such a rock star?"

"Rayanne Miller, are you giving me a compliment?"

"Fuck off," I reply, rolling my eyes at him, and Caleb laughs at me. "That note's not an easy one to hit. I'm surprised you added them to Spotify for all the world to see."

"It's Isla," Caleb shrugs. "She blasts it on the radio every time we're in the car together."

"Or basically anytime she turns on music," I groan, conceding the point while simultaneously rolling my eyes at Isla. "Look, I like these guys, and this song is fucking catchy. But if I keep listening to them for much longer, I think my soul might turn bright pink or into a fucking rainbow that drains my soul."

"Yeah, rainbow souls are the fucking devil," Caleb snorts at me. I look at him mockingly devastated, catching his eye. We both laugh, and then he starts singing again, and I—damn my eyes—start clapping along.

"Fuck this shit," I curse the Jonas Brothers. "I need to darken my soul some more."

I find The Clash on Caleb's liked songs and the car ride becomes companionable again. Caleb and I find our comfort zone, singing, poking fun at each other, and before I know it, we're at my apartment. Caleb jumps out of his truck, and I join him.

"Here, let me." he begins, and works on undoing the straps securing the tree. "I'm going to drag it out of the bed, and we'll test out how much weight you can support, okay?"

"Sounds good," I reply, ready and eager to prove that the tree's weight isn't as bad as Caleb thinks it is. It's big, I know. But it's going to be gorgeous in my living room. Caleb drags it out of the bed, and I grab my keys and phone, securing them in my back pocket.

"Do you have a good spot to hold on to?" Caleb asks. "This should work here." He gestures for me to fall in place as he grips the tree about a foot down from the top.

"Yeah, I got it," I say, mimicking his hand position in the tree. His shoulders brush against mine and heat rises in my cheeks, unbidden at the touch. As we make eye contact, the lock of hair falls down his face, obstructing his vision. It's begging me to brush it out of the way. Caleb's lips curl into a half smile, and before I can react, he's shifted his stance behind me. He lifts the trunk of the tree, and the weight isn't as bad as I expected. "This is good. Let's go."

"Hold on," Caleb says, dropping his end of the tree on the ground.

"It's *fine*, Caleb," I groan. "Let's just get the tree in the apartment."

"I'm grabbing these just in case," he replies, snatching the straps. "I don't think we'll need them, but I want them handy."

"*Okay* Caleb," I whine. "Let's go!" We take our positions and make our way to the staircase. We ascend the first flight smoothly, which quickly become a hazard as we climb higher. My apartment complex has stairwells that are narrow with sharp, awkward turns that make the positioning of my arms and will power wear down quickly as Caleb navigates the corners. By the time we get to the middle of the second stairwell, sweat is dampening my bra, and my tank under my sweater is clinging to the small of my back.

Caleb doesn't look much better. His face is a mask of concentration, bearing the weight of the heaviest part of the tree.

"Why are you stopping?" Caleb grunts, "This fucker's heavy."

"Sorry, sorry," I apologize, fanning myself with my sweater. "It's just my sweater. It's hot with this thing on."

"I told you," Caleb huffs. "Why didn't you change before?"

"I have a fucking tank on, alright!?" I snap. I haven't forgotten that smirk he gave me at the suggestion I take off my sweater earlier this morning. He may have been right, but I'll be damned before I admit it to him just now.

I grab the top of the tree and we drag it to the top of the second story. Caleb releases the trunk, and it lands with a heavy thunk on the ground. My hands are sticky with sap and fuzz from my sweater which sticks to my palms.

Great, I groan internally. It's got to be done though, so I lift my sweater off. The suppressed weight of heat is lifted, and I'm instantly relieved. I attempt to brush my hands on my jeans and tuck my sweater into my elbow to secure it.

I'm about to tell Caleb I'm ready to conquer the last flight of stairs but am caught off guard by the way he is openly staring at me. His breath is heavy from catching it, and there's an unrestrained look of wanting in his eyes. With the way his hair falls in his face, his mouth stern with concentration, Caleb looks like a different man. The way he studies my exposed skin sends shivers up my spine.

I'm used to the teenager Caleb looking at me with puppy dog eyes. I'm used to the dopey kid trying to catch Isla and me unaware of his presence, surprising us in her bedroom. I'm used to the kid reaching out for my hand, seeking help.

I am not used to this full-grown man eyeing me like I'm a prized treasure. I'm not used to feeling my cheeks blush under his attention—which they most *definitely* are not. And I'm *definitely* not used to liking the way he studies me when my clothes come off.

What just happened?

This is Caleb. I admonish myself. *Remember? Isla's kid brother. Girl code demands that she comes first.*

"Come on," I break the spell, and toss my sweater on the ground. "I'll come back for it."

"Yeah, okay." Caleb replies, his voice filled with sensuality.

Did he just say it like that on purpose? The two words send shivers up my spine. I gather the tree in my grip and chance one more glance at him. Caleb's steady look of concentration is still laced with desire. A thought slides into place as I groan internally.

Oh.

Oh my god.

Has he been checking me out this whole time? Should we change positions so I'm not getting checked out by my best friend's little brother? I curse silently, wondering what it is that I've gotten myself into exactly. If I'd caught him staring at me before hauling this nine-and-a-half-foot monstrosity up the stairwell, I could have insisted upon swapping places. But it's too late now and I'm fucking exhausted.

"Come on, Miller." Caleb groans, lifting the trunk of the tree. "Let's get this done with."

I lift up the end of my tree and carry on, but I'm so distracted that I stumble at least three times up the stairwell. I can't get over the idea that Caleb might be watching my ass every step we take to my apartment. I'm shaken by this man and the way he's been staring at me.

This will be fine. It's not a big deal.

It's a big deal.

I'm totally wrong because if I think about seeing that chiseled jaw flex with concentration one more time, I'll be into it. And then I'm going to have to seriously examine what the fuck is going on in my mind.

Ray, get your head in the game! I admonish myself. *Not. Now.*

"Ray," Caleb's voice is steady with concern. "Focus. We're almost there!"

"Sorry," I reply, and I steady my left hand on the railing the last few steps. When we get the tree up the stairwell, we both drop it with relief. I grab the keys from my back pocket and open the door.

"I'll just grab some water, okay?"

Caleb's jaw flexes in acknowledgement as he nods, letting me know that he's heard me. I clench my fist, resisting my reaction to that small movement. Is it just me, or is there still desire lingering in that look he's giving me?

When did I start paying attention to every small movement Caleb makes? I can't remain still, eager to retreat back to my kitchen with the excuse of doing something. I gather myself back together while I fill two cups of water.

Does Caleb like ice?

Should I even care?

Whatever.

I open the freezer door and throw ice in one of glasses. As I make my way back to Caleb, I find him studying the tree and the doorway.

"Here," I say, startling him. "Pick one."

Caleb takes the one without ice, which is good because I prefer extra cold water. We down our glasses, and the tightness of my muscles relaxes.

"Do you want more?" I ask, my voice unsure and unsteady. Nothing like my usual self. *What the fuck, Rayanne?*

"No, this is great, thanks." Caleb says. I watch him take my cup and walk into my kitchen, placing them in the sink. Are his shoulders broader than when he arrived to pick me up this morning? And why are his jeans hanging lower than I remember?

When did Caleb Gardiner become so sexy?

There are so many problems making themselves apparent; my fingers are still tingling from his touch, and I love the way he just walked right into my kitchen to put the dishes in the sink. Caleb could have just handed them to me to deal with later, but he's taken action for himself and done something nice for me in the process.

Fuck. That's sexy too.

"Hey Ray," Caleb greets me from the kitchen. "I'm going to go grab the ladder from the back of my truck. Want me to grab your sweater?"

"That'd be great." I offer him a small smile. "Thanks."

Caleb nods his head in acceptance, and I watch him walk out the door. Do I shamelessly check out his ass as he goes down the stairs, picks up my sweater, and heads back to the truck?

Yes. Yes, I do.

I'm not so blasé that Caleb could catch me as he heads back to the truck though. I retreat to the kitchen, grab one of the cups in the sink and fill it with water then steadily down it. I breathe in deeply and exhale, taking a moment for myself. I come back to myself slowly with some water and a couple deep breaths. I try to reign in the madness that is my mind and all the ways my thoughts circle back to Caleb. This time, when I tell myself that he isn't sexy—that I don't have the brain space to think of him as anything except a friend and Isla's brother, I almost believe it.

Almost.

Today has been… well, it's been trouble. Spending all this time with Caleb alone is trouble. Just exactly how long has it been since I saw him? Was it last month for Thanksgiving?

That day was really great. Graham and his sister joined us

for the holiday since they live in the States. I sat across from Caleb and enjoyed the meal with all the Gardiners and my family in town. It was loud with ten conversations going on at once. In all the madness, I found small moments with Caleb that I was grateful for. We shared quiet glances at each other as we laughed at others, delighting in a good meal. When I dove into the chocolate pecan pie Caleb made, I remember watching him study my reaction like my opinion of the dessert was the only one that mattered.

That look was so similar to what I just experienced when I took my sweater off. I hadn't caught on then, but I understand it much better now. Caleb's feelings—this crush—it hasn't changed. He's not over it, but he's gotten better at masking his feelings.

And now I'm discovering that I actually *like* that look he gives me.

Fuck!

I am in so much trouble.

"We have a problem, Rayanne." Caleb calls out from outside the apartment. I jump in surprise, not prepared for what will happen next. I glance up, feeling like a deer in headlights. Caleb stands taller, his shoulders broader. I take the last sip of water from my cup, then place it in the sink.

We sure do have a problem.

God, he looks good.

"Oh, yeah?" I reply, shaking my head again. I need to get out of my headspace now.

Caleb navigates walking around the tree with the ladder, lifting it up slightly and placing it against one of the walls in the hallway. The position of his shirt and the slight slouch of his pants reveal an angle that leads down to the V of his crotch. My toes involuntarily curl inside my boots as I clench my thighs together. Just that little exposure of skin and I feel my body melting into putty.

God, what would Isla think of me? I turn away so I don't shamelessly stare, but the image is burned into my eye sockets now.

"Yeah, we got a problem." Caleb replies, stepping in close and into my space. He turns so we're making eye contact and tosses my sweater at me. I hug it like it's my support blanket. He grins at me and my heart flutters at the sweep of his hair and that troublesome smirk. Caleb's musk is distracting, and I have to restrain myself from lifting my head up to the crook of his neck so I can determine what exactly lies under his scent.

"What's that?" I ask, my voice heady with the lingering thoughts taunting me.

"I'm not sure the tree is going to fit through your doorway."

rayanne

LITTLE DID I KNOW | JULIA MICHAELS

"What do you mean, the tree won't fit!?" I exclaim. Gone is the thrill of that sexy musk. Gone is my insecurity. This is impossible. I couldn't exactly measure at the tree farm, but I reviewed the size of my doorway repeatedly to make sure this didn't happen when I did pick my tree.

"I mean," Caleb begins, rather impatiently. "That the bottom of your tree is too fucking full to fit through the door."

"Impossible," I reply, my anger feeding off Caleb's impatience. "It has to fit. I bought one that would."

"Yeah, *sweetheart*, this isn't a single-family home," Caleb retorts. "It's a fucking apartment complex, and the door to this apartment is not as wide as a five bedroom in Westlake. Your tree is just too fucking big to get inside."

The *sweetheart* is not a term of affection, and I'm not stupid enough to assume it is. I focus on maintaining my composure as a tiny thrill tightens in my gut. I need to resist the urge to get in his face, only because I don't know what the outcome would be if I did. Neither of us back down, and the tension between us escalates. My feet remain grounded as I resolve to never discover if taking that step forward would result in a shove or kissing. *Not that I want to kiss Caleb or anything...*

Definitely not.

"You're wrong," I declare. "You must be. Isn't there some ordinance about door size regulation in Austin? There has to be." I know, because I looked them up. I shove Caleb out of the way and examine the problem myself. I have an eye for creating vision and selling the hell out of it. I can make this damn tree fit in my apartment.

Admittedly, I can understand why Caleb thinks it won't fit. Even with the tree contained by the net, the sheer size is much bigger at the bottom than it looks. I retrieve one of the measuring tapes Isla left lying on my kitchen island and pace back to the entryway. Caleb smirks at me, confirming my suspicions. I may not have had a tape at the farm, but this beauty was here with me before I left this morning, and I know my measurements. This is just for ceremony for Caleb fucking Gardiner, current pain in my ass. I take his hand and hold it in place as I pointedly take the door's measurements.

"Stay." I command, directing Caleb. I pull tight on the

52

measuring tape and crouch down to be precise. "Thirty-two inches. Let's look at the tree."

Caleb is now openly entertained by my need for precision. We measure the width of the tree with the tape, and even though it looks like a tight fit, I know it'll work. "It's going to be fine Caleb." I smile up at him. "It's within an inch difference, but it's going to work. We may have to shove really hard though."

He laughs and offers me a hand up. Caleb lets go once I'm steady on my feet, but the impression of his hand around mine remains. I brush my hand against my jeans to remove the feeling, but the sensation sticks.

Don't think too hard about how those smooth callouses felt warm and comforting. Don't—

Stop it!

I look up at Caleb watching me, smirking. Is he just messing with me? I'm beginning to suspect that his impatience is all just a show. Even when he argues and gets in my face, I know Caleb still wants me. My new awareness of him isn't doing me any favors. Now that I'm aware, I know a knife could cut the sexual tension in the air between us. It's unsettling.

I stand taller, resisting acknowledgment. I'm not here for this internal conflict trying to take over. Caleb has one job, and that's to help me get my tree into my apartment and secure it into the stand. I don't need all these extra feelings creeping up on me, attempting to slowly take over my mind.

Not now.

"Come on," he grins. "Let's shove this tree through the doorway." We reposition the tree so that we can push it through, me in the front guiding the way.

"Wait up," I say, dropping the tree so I can assess the space in my living room. I shift around my side and coffee tables and Caleb joins me in time to help lift the coffee table and move it to the side.

"Do you think we need to move the couch?" I muse, keeping my focus, my gaze, and thoughts on the task at hand.

"There's no way that the tree and both of us are fitting in this apartment without moving it." Caleb replies. I huff in protest as we move it towards my kitchen. Caleb surveys the now very open living room. "Where's your tree stand?"

"It's in the closet." I reply. "I'll go get it."

I leave to get the tree stand from my bedroom closet, and when I return Caleb quirks his lips with amusement, then breaks into laughter.

"Rayanne, what the fuck is that?" he's asks, still doubled over with amusement.

"It's my tree stand," I reply, refusing to see what's so funny.

"Yeah, for a six-footer," he answers, "Not this monstrosity."

"It is not a monstrosity!" I reply, stomping my foot.

"Come on, let's get the beast in here," Caleb snorts his amusement once more.

"Fuck off, Gardiner." I mutter. I position the tree stand in front of the bay windows, which look out to a gorgeous view of the ever-growing Austin city skyline. It wasn't this tall ten years ago, but with the way the population keeps growing, it won't change anytime soon. It's still a beautiful sight and I've daydreamed about this scenery with my perfect Christmas tree in the foreground for months.

"Today, Ray." Caleb singsongs at me while snapping his fingers impatiently at me. "Let's get this fucker in here, eh?"

I scowl at Caleb, annoyed at his finger snapping. When I get back to him, I shove his shoulder. "Don't snap your fingers at me, asshole." I grumble. I snap my fingers back at him, and he grins his entertainment.

"Do you like that, Caleb Gardiner?" I demand, hoping he hates it as much as I do.

"I had to get your attention somehow." Caleb stills my hand with his, but the warmth that spreads through my body is as unwelcome as it is pleasant. I scoff at his argument and the swirling emotions shifting inside me, but Caleb keeps moving to the base of the tree. "Right, on my count, we'll push and pull the tree through your door at the same time."

"I'm pulling." I confirm, also moving into position. Caleb offers me such a lazy, knowing grin that my cheeks flush pink. I ignore my embarrassment as I bend my knees down and position one hand in front of the other on the top of the tree. *One… two…*

"Three!" Caleb shouts, and he shoves as I pull the tree into the front of my foyer. The force with which he pushes the tree into the apartment pushes me down on my ass and I'm lost under the tree. "Fuck! Rayanne!"

I burst into laughter and instantly regret it. Needles are in my face, my hair, and my mouth. My shirt is shoved up and the sharpness of the tree needles prickle my skin. Caleb's footsteps approach as he tosses the tree aside and offers me a hand up. He steadies me with a strong grasp on my forearms, then he looks me over once I'm steady. I tug my shirt down and spit pine needles out of my mouth.

"Jesus, Rayanne." Caleb runs his fingers through my hair, dislodging needles. "Are you okay?"

"I'm fine," I reply, unable to control my giggling. "God, I must look like the Christmas Tree Mistress from Hell."

"Nah," Caleb beams down at me with a wide, generous smile dancing with open amusement. There's nothing cynical or biting in his glance, and my breath catches. His hands are gently woven into my hair and the sides of his eyes are crinkled with amusement. Caleb's hair falls in his eyes, and that base instinct I have to brush his hair out of his eyes tests my every reserve.

There's a loud, busy energy about Caleb that doesn't always match the man I see. It comes from the need to keep everything light, I suspect. He edged close to destruction once a few years ago, making both Isla and me worried. That loud, questioning, cynical side to Caleb showcases what could be some form of deflection for any feelings he wants to keep close to his sleeve. There isn't much stillness about Caleb for the most part, but when he finds those moments, I know they are precious to him. Just as the precision needed for baking helps him find that stillness in his mind. I haven't seen it for myself, but Isla's told me several times.

The air settles between us as our eyes lock on each other. His hands remain curled in the tips of my hair and his gaze steady on me. This moment has calmed between us, and we're quiet together. He's slowed down and settled to one task. Caleb is simply breathtaking in his stillness.

I'm the task, I muse internally. *He's tending to my well-being. Is this what it would always be like between us?*

The thought is unbidden, but it's made its mark. Like so many moments throughout the day, I'm reconsidering how much I don't know Caleb Gardiner now. I'm beginning to suspect that I have no inkling of how deep his feelings for me really are. I'm not sure how much I want to accept the depth of those feelings pointed in my direction.

When Caleb breaks away from me, the space between us is tangible. In haste, I look around for something to do and my eyes settle on the beast of a tree in my front room.

Oh God…

It looms large in the middle of my apartment even contained in the netting. I run back to the tree stand and where I've positioned it, then move it about four inches forward. Is that enough? I scoot it up another two inches, then step back, trying to predict the space needed for this over-whelming tree.

"Rayanne," Caleb begins, and I turn to him. "Is the tree stand in position?" In the time that I've been recalculating the tree size and positioning it in front of the window, Caleb has centered himself over the tree and is slowly inching it back towards me.

"Put that down!" I yell at him. "Don't be a fucking idiot. We can drag it to the base then lift it up into the stand." Caleb scoffs as he singlehandedly shoves and drags the tree across my living room, despite my protestations. He rotates it with ease, leaving me with my mouth gaping open. That was a seriously impressive show of sheer physical strength.

"Are you going to be able to support the weight of it while I lock the tree into the stand?" Caleb asks, brow raised in question.

"Yeah," I reply, "It shouldn't be that hard."

"You're going to have to keep it still, alright?" Caleb says, a cheeky smile flirting on his lips.

"Yeah, I got it." I say, snorting with impatience. We both push the tree up and he maneuvers it to a standing position then stands up to assess its placement in the tree stand.

"Here." he begins, and his body envelops mine from my back as he positions my hands for securing the tree. Caleb's body is warm with his large, smoothed, calloused hands surrounding mine. The heat of his touch spreads through my body, and I have to steady my breaths to fight the urge to clench my legs together.

"You have to stay absolutely still," Caleb murmurs, leaning down. His mouth is far too close for comfort. He repositions my hands for the right placement to keep the tree straight. Caleb's own hands are huge and envelop mine. I lean further into the netting and hold tighter as I reposition my legs to support my new stance. I clear my voice, trying to dislodge Caleb.

"Yeah, Caleb—I got it." I snap, louder than I intend.

"Good. Stay there," he replies, doubtful about my grip. He leans down to turn the first screw into the trunk. The full heat of his body rests on my side, and I hug the tree to fight the sensation of his touch. My cheeks burn red as I realize that if we readjusted our positions, his face would rest right at my crotch. I tighten my grip on the tree as I try not to examine why exactly my legs clench together.

Caleb is focused on his task, but his insistent touch seduces me with unexpected warmth and is doing incredible things to my imagination. He raises his eyes to me with a look of steady concentration. He rests his chin on my thigh, and instead of dismissing his puppy dog eyes like I might have before, they become endearing to me. Insane, impulsive urges tell me to abandon the tree so I can discover just how many ways he can touch my thighs. What would those broad hands feel like, resting high on my legs? I gasp quietly, trying to control my spiraling thoughts.

Spoiler alert: it's not working.

"Ray, you gotta keep the tree still." Caleb lectures, a knowing smile teasing me.

"I am." I snap back.

"You are not," he says. "It keeps swaying side to side."

"Sorry!" I reply, hugging the tree tighter, praying that it will stay in place. I lean my head in to keep it steady, and Caleb works as quickly as he can around the tree to secure it. When the torture is finished, we both stand back.

"Ray," Caleb says, tone amused and sardonic. "You're going to have a tree falling out of that stand any minute."

"The hell I am," I retort, definitely sharper than intended.

58

Whatever magic Caleb has woven into the moment has disappeared as he begins insulting the tree standing in my apartment.

"If it lasts longer than two hours in that stand without falling, I'll be shocked." Caleb pronounces, nothing short of sarcastic.

"Well, it's positioned straight, right?" I demand. "It's not going to fall?"

"Of course, it's not going to fall," Caleb scoffs. "I've been putting up Christmas trees for ten years." The tree is straight, and for all his questioning, it looks fine. Caleb begins to laugh.

"What?" I ask. "The tree's sturdy."

Caleb shakes his head and begins moving my furniture back into place. I lend a hand with the coffee table and couch. He finally gestures at the tree when we've moved the furniture back in place. It overshadows the rest of the living room, and I haven't even cut the netting off yet. He raises an eyebrow at me in question, but I am determined not to acknowledge it.

I head back into the kitchen instead to grab my scissors so I can begin releasing the tree from its netting. I start at the base and work my way up until I'm about a third of the way from the top. More than a head taller than me, Caleb smirks, grabs the scissors and finishes the job. He refuses to move out of my space; his arms reach higher as he cuts the netting away. With each snip of the scissors, his body brushes against mine, and the raw connection between us begins to weave a sort of magic between us once more.

Caleb looks down at me when he finishes. Indulgence dances in his eyes and his smile is so inviting. He leans in, and I swear to god, he's going to kiss me. It's etched there, right on his stupid face. Clearly entertained, Caleb is unabashed with his wanting of me. I'm just not prepared to acknowledge or accept what I know now. Between the buildup of my unwanted interest and Caleb Gardiner just being *here*, my stamina may not last much longer. I escape to the kitchen and fill up a pitcher with water and he follows me then steadies the pitcher in my hands as I attempt to fill it with water.

"Ray," he breathes my name out, and *god,* it's delicious. Full of wanting and desire, the syllable resonates through my body, and I want to look up. When I don't respond, he brushes hair out of my eyes and picks out a few remaining needles. "You're a mess."

It's an excuse to keep touching, and I'm itching to give into the game he's playing.

You can't. I reprimand. *This is Isla's little brother.*

"Caleb," I say, closing my eyes. I have to shut this down fast. His touch is so inviting and he's so close, but if I look up at him, he's going to fucking kiss me. I'm not prepared to open that door. I still the movement of his hands in my hair with my own.

"We can't do this." I finally breathe out.

"Do what?" he asks, a smile in his tone. "We aren't doing anything."

What a fucking liar.

"Caleb," I try again, more insistent this time. I drag his fingers from my hair and release them gently. "Thank you for the help. I really couldn't have gotten my tree up without you."

But you have to go.

The look Caleb gives me is nothing short of affection: attentive, kind, and patient. His attention is focused and singular. The open affection is so… weird. I'm not used to being the center of attention—not like this. I shut my eyes, willing the man in front of me to turn back into that awkward preteen I knew how to handle. But it's no good.

60

Caleb isn't a kid anymore.

"Fine," he says playfully, and steps out of my space. Relief washes over me. "I'll see you when the tree falls over."

"The tree isn't falling over!" I stomp my foot with anger, feeling too frustrated to care about that indecent, perilous moment where I might have begun to fall under Caleb's spell.

My tree is fine. It will be *just* fine. "Keep the ladder for decorations." he says and messes up my hair like the stupid kid brother he is. Needles fall down my shirt, and I swat at him in retaliation. "Call me when shit falls apart." He winks at me and opens the door.

"Fuck off, Gardiner!" I yell back at him. Caleb laughs as he closes the door. I'm so tempted to throw something at him to make my point. Instead, I curse out loudly and walk back to my kitchen to fill the tree with water. When I'm finished with the task, I stand back in my living room to take in the tree and immediately start cursing in fluent sailor again. The tree is just too fucking big, even without decorations.

Motherfucking Caleb, I'm going to bloody *kill* him.

Wait.

Maybe I can fix it.

Perhaps if I rearrange the furniture, I can create more space. I try a few arrangements, moving the big furniture around so frequently that I'm a hot sweaty mess. I blast the AC and strip down to my underwear. A puddle of tree needles falls at my feet, and I groan at all the different messes that need cleaning.

Whatever, I groan internally. *I'll fix it later*. I have bigger fish to fry at the moment.

No matter the layout of my furniture, it's all a fucking catastrophe. The tree takes up all my walking space, even if I shift it to the side. The best variation features my couch facing the window and one of my chairs next to the tree, with the other kitty corner to the left, but my living room is simply all too confining.

The tree will be beautiful when it's decorated, but right now I'm too exhausted to consider the task of even stringing the lights. I curse Caleb again, because he's right. But I'll be damned if I'm saying a word to him about that.

rayanne

AS IT WAS | HARRY STYLES

A resounding whoosh disrupts the air, followed by a loud echoing sound of clunks clanging against hard surfaces. Then there's a strange sweeping motion. Melodic bells chime the final note of the peculiar song, and I sit up in bed, blinking stupidly. I turn my head to the side, listening as closely as I can; the tinkling bells transform into sounds of glass plopping, then breaking. I stand up immediately, panic building at the odd symphony reverberating through my apartment.

Tinkling bells crashing? In my sleep hazed state, I'm not even sure I know what that means. I fumble into my closet, grab my combat boots and stumble into them. When I walk past the table beside my bed, I curl my fingers reflexively around my phone and AirPods. As I turn the corner into my living room, the tinkling glass makes a lot more sense.

Time has slowed as I gaze at my magnificent, half-dressed Christmas tree that lies horizontal as it rests across my coffee table and my living room couch. The decorations I so carefully placed in all the right places last night now bounce precariously from the Christmas tree. The sweet ring of bells are the ornaments that have lost their place from the force of falling off the tree. I wince as I watch the Christmas candles topple out of their holders. The sound of trickling water catches my attention, and I watch with horror as the water creeps closer to me. The Christmas lights I obsessively placed are now half immersed in water.

I realize, very quickly, that all the dreams this tree promised once are quickly becoming the things of nightmares. As time speeds back into real time, reality taps me smartly on the ass, and I'm hurled from the Twilight Zone.

"Shit! Shit! Shit!" I curse, running into action towards the wall, then pulling the plug on the fairy lights. "Fuck!" I stamp towards my linen closet, then grab every towel I have to stop the water from soaking into the carpet. If the damage ruins the carpet, I'm entirely fucked. Even with panic rising in my body, I take the time to exhale slowly and calculate the best locations for towels. Ornaments crunch under my boots as I place each towel, and I wince involuntarily.

Fuck. What do I do next?

The tree has been standing in place for three days and I *thought* this situation was under control. I expected to have the advantage enough to tell Caleb "I told you so" so I could laugh in his face. But as I take in my too large Christmas tree, absorbing just how disproportionately small the tree stand is,

I realize how much I vastly overrated my confidence. Laughter bubbles up from inside, coming out bitter.

Fucking Caleb Gardiner. I'll be damned if I call him for help. I can't handle his knowing tone if I call him now. I do the next best thing and call Isla. As I tell Siri to dial her number, I check my phone for the time. It's three o'clock in the afternoon in London. It'll be fine. Girl code dictates all emergency calls be answered at any time of the day.

"Ray?" Isla asks, brows furrowed, instantly noting my distress. "Are you okay?"

"I am not *fucking okay*." I moan, dragging my fingers through my hair. "Look at this fucking mess I'm in!" I change the camera point of view to show the god damned catastrophe, and I hear her surprised gasp.

"Ray!" Isla's tone makes me squirm as I show her the impending disaster in my living room. "Ray, turn the phone around." I whine involuntarily, stomping my foot like a child in a tantrum when I hear her distress. "First off—are you okay?" Isla demands.

"I'm fine." I admit tersely. "But my apartment is not. Jesus Isla, where do I start!?"

"Did you get towels yet?"

"Yeah," I reply, flipping the camera view to show the apartment. "I've done what I can to prevent the worst of it, but the towels are already soaking up the water, and there are crushed ornaments everywhere."

"Rayanne?" It's Graham chiming in. Of course, he's with her. What did I expect? She's in London meeting his family and friends, so of course he's here for my humiliation.

"Hey Graham." I deadpan.

"Hey," I hear the catch of amusement in his tone. I know how devastatingly handsome that grin is, so I pull my phone back into face range so I can see it. Graham towers over Isla, both sharing mirrored expressions of concern.

"Are you safe?" Graham asks. "Are you wearing shoes?"

"I have my combat boots on." I reply, then point my camera at my feet with my mismatched combat boots and pajama pants. "See?"

"Good." Graham sounds relieved. "How big is the tree? I ask, because you'll need to get it off the furniture and floor as soon as possible."

"It's uh…" I stall, exhaling a deep breath slowly. I might be getting a lecture from Isla at any moment by now. Why I thought it was a good idea to call her, I'll never know.

"What did you do?" Isla's tone is slightly accusatory as she narrows her eyes at me, knowing just how obsessive I can get with my Christmas decorations.

It's a family trait, alright? I can't help it.

"What do you mean, what did I do?" I narrow my eyes in return. "I don't think I like that tone, Isla Gardiner."

"You know *exactly* what the fuck I'm talking about," Isla replies, raising a brow at me. "Your Christmas tree has face-planted into the furniture. I know how your mind works, missy. Did you balance out the decorations when putting them on the tree?"

"No."

"Did you overwater the Christmas tree?"

"…Maybe." I didn't think too hard about the extra water I added to my tree stand last night, but perhaps that was the literal tipping point? I fucking sigh.

"How big is that tree, Ray?" Isla asks, and the sound of her voice makes me look at the camera. Isla and Graham look at me with solemn grimaces in anticipation to my answers.

"It's, uhh," I falter, shamed for my overenthusiastic vision. "Stupidly big."

"Fuck, Rayanne." Isla sounds exasperated. "What exactly did you do?"

"Look it's fine, I'll figure it out." I deflect, instantly

regretting my call to Isla. I don't want to admit to another Gardiner how much I fucked up. I didn't realize how much I would be adjusting to how large this Christmas tree is, even after three days of it looming in my apartment. I had to shove the furniture around and pull the tree farther from the window so I could walk around the tree as I put lights on it. It took me two days and that godforsaken ladder Caleb left me. I huff with exasperation.

"Show me the goddamned Christmas tree," Isla demands. "Please tell me you did not buy a nine-footer. Your ceilings are tall, but they aren't that tall. It's barely going to fit—"

"It's actually nine and a half feet," I grumble, then huff.

"Rayanne Lee Miller!" Isla yells, and I hear the echoing impact of her foot stomping the ground in London. "Stop being so fucking stubborn and show me the damn tree."

I cave in with a devastated sigh and turn the FaceTime footage to show the tree in my living room again.

"Damnit, Ray." Isla sounds furious. "Why the fuck would you buy such a big Christmas tree?"

"Because it's beautiful?" I offer.

"Rayanne," Graham observes with such delicate precision that he doesn't sound amused. "You do understand that tree is taking up half your living room, right?"

"Shut it, Graham," I grumble as he chuckles. "Just tell me how to get this asshole tree up off the furniture, please. I'll also accept advice for the conversation with my landlord, so I don't get evicted."

"How exactly did you get this tree in your apartment?" Isla grins with amusement.

"Caleb helped," I reluctantly admit.

"Caleb?" Isla's familiar amused tone makes me grimace. Her brows rise above her eyebrows as she looks at Graham, and they share a knowing look I do not like at all.

"Look, Niels and Thomas are out of town with their families," I sigh. "And mom and dad left for Copenhagen for Christmas a week and a half ago. I literally had no one else, since you were in Arizona working…"

"You called Caleb?" Isla's amusement is evident. Our established Girl Code clearly dictates brothers are off limits, but Isla never seems to object the idea of my relationship with Caleb changing. I ignore her inviting tone to spill the details. When I don't respond, she presses again.

"Caleb, my little brother?"

"He was the only person available to help," I grumble. "Everyone was gone."

"Ray, you do understand the man would literally do anything for you, right?" Graham asks, his tone lilted with slight exasperation. Isla's smile is wide, and I'm ready to tap the red button on my phone to end the call.

Yes, I know. I know with the new seeing eyes that understand *just* how much Caleb cares for me. And for the first time, I'm nearly indulgent with Isla's heavy-handed hints because my position on the matter is shifting against my will. I'm aware that this is my best friend's little brother, someone I've watched grow up. I'm aware of how much these feelings are catching up with me.

I'm aware.

"Look," I sigh. The delay in my response has Isla looking at Graham with surprise, and he nods, acknowledging it too. I don't want to know whatever it is they've discovered in my silence. I move on quickly before they can say another word. I exaggerate my sigh, trying to press my point, "Look, if you two lovebirds can't help me figure this shit out, I'll do it on my own. I just need to get this tree off my furniture. I don't need Caleb—"

"The physical body weight of that tree suggests otherwise," Graham notes, rather dryly. I narrow my eyes at his insinuation. I do not need that British sass right now. I'm about to press my thumb on the end button when Isla and Graham begin to have a silent conversation. It couldn't have been more than a few seconds, but it feels like a lifetime as he looks into the phone and smiles his farewell. "I'll let you two sort this out. Ray, I wish you luck."

"Bye," I reply, the bitterness of my tone not quite hidden.

"Babes," Isla begins, voice tentative. She pauses once more as she watches Graham leave. When she turns back to look at me, she has the expression of a saint fixed on her features. I groan internally. Isla's about to walk me through exactly what I don't want to think about. "You know that even if you could get the tree up yourself, it's going to take all day to get this shit cleaned up, right?"

"Yes," I sigh.

"And your towels are most likely absorbed to maximum capacity. If not now, then they will be, certainly very soon." Isla uses her soothing voice that always seems to work magic on me.

"Probably," I sigh. God, she always gets her point across when she does this with me.

"And you'll be spending all day doing shit work alone when you know you need to replace what's lost, right?" Isla's brow raises with the leading question, and I fucking take the bait.

"Yeah." I sigh, resigned.

"Then call Caleb." Isla urges.

"Do I *have* to!?" I whine. "God, he's going to be *such* an asshole about this. You should have seen him Isla—"

"Caleb knows exactly what your family is like with Christmas."

"And what does that mean?!" I demand, narrowing my eyes.

"Rayanne," Isla rolls her eyes at me. "Don't be ridiculous. Your family is practically royalty around Austin when it

71

comes to Christmas decorations. We all know the sort of Christmases you grew up with. And *you*, Rayanne Lee Miller, are a romantic. We only have a week to go before Christmas, and the fact that you don't have your decorations up now is most likely eating you alive."

"I really hate that you know me this well." I grumble.

"Look," Isla smiles an apologetic smile. "I wish I could be there to help, but—"

"You're with Graham," I cut her off. "You're living your best life with that gorgeous Englishman of yours."

"I am." Isla beams in the way I only associate with Graham these days. She deserves this happiness with him.

"How's it going?" I ask, dying to know.

"Nice try," Isla narrows her gaze at me accusingly. "While I'm thrilled to be here, and while I love meeting all of Graham's friends and family, that is not why you called."

Damn. I thought I could get away with that diversion.

"Ray," Isla begins, tentatively. "Talk to me. Did something happen with Caleb?"

"Not really?" I sigh, and the question in my tone gives me away.

"What happened?" Isla asks, eyes dancing with entertainment.

"*Nothing!*" I exclaim, shifting uncomfortably in my position. I look over to the couch, tempted to sit down, but I'd only be crowded in by the tree. I sigh, giving up as I look at my best friend in the phone. "At least not really. But it's been a while since I've seen Caleb and…"

"*And!?*" Isla's unconcealed excitement digs in my side.

"*Why* are you so excited?" I grumble. "He's your brother, and you know what girl code dictates."

"Rayanne," Isla replies with a cool, steadying tone. "That was always your rule—not mine. Has something shifted?"

72

"It is not! You never looked twice at Thomas or Niels when we were growing up!" I exclaim defensively.

"That's because they were at least eight years older than us and I wasn't interested," Isla smirks. "You were the one always insisting Caleb was off limits."

I open my mouth to protest, but then all my memories come flooding back, recognizing that Isla was always rather silent on this girl code. Does this mean what I think it does? Is Isla correct and I've been protesting too loudly for a reason?

I sigh, resigned, caught between the new revelations and the need to retreat from my feelings inside. Tuesday was already intense, if only because I'm beginning to *see* Caleb's gaze on me and all that comes with those implications. My newfound physical reaction to his regard for me is unsettling. Caleb has grown up well, and I noticed *all* the changes.

"It *did*!" Isla is triumphant.

"Isla," I hesitate, finally showing some of my inner conflict. "I don't know about this. We've known each other for so long, and he's—"

"Honestly, I don't care," Isla interrupts. She lets out a little squeal of excitement and jumps up and down like a little kid. When she finally catches the surprise on my face, she turns serious again. "Look, I never missed how y'all leaned on each other when I couldn't be there. And you two work well together—you always have. I *like* you and Caleb together."

"I don't know," I falter. "I don't like spending time alone with him. I don't know what will happen if we continue to spend more time together." Isla's grin is triumphant at that revelation. "Isla!" I moan.

"Look babes, I got your back either way, regardless of what I think *should* happen." Isla soothes. "I love you both. But whether you like it or not, you need Caleb right now. The disaster that is now your apartment needs help. If you want the Christmas vision of your dreams, you're going to need to clean and replace everything that's been damaged."

I sigh, resigned. "Fine."

"Do me a favor, Ray," Isla catches my eye, and the tone in her voice is conciliatory and demanding at the same time. "Ask yourself what you want. Whatever is shifting or changing between you two, don't hide from it. That's not the Rayanne I know. Forget about me and Caleb and just focus on what you want. If you find yourself in a position where you don't want to fight the chemistry between y'all, then don't. You don't *need* my blessing, but you have it all the same."

"Isla—"

"I mean it." Isla promises, cutting off my interruptions. "Find your happiness. If that's with Caleb, I'm okay with it, alright?"

"Yeah," I sigh. "Not sure it was needed, but thanks anyway."

I really needed it.

"Good." Isla replies, cutting me a look that tells me she knows exactly what I need. "Call Caleb. If he's an asshole about it, I'll kick his ass later."

I smirk, "I can handle his shit. Thanks, Isla. I love you."

"Love you too babes," Isla blows me a kiss. "Take care of you and that ridiculous Christmas tree of yours."

"It is *not ridiculous*," I narrow my eyes. The last thing I hear is my best friend's laughter and I grimace. She clearly thinks I'm bullshitting. I'm tempted to say fuck all to the annoying Gardiners in my life and fix everything myself.

I can do this shit on my own, right?

Right.

I work for an hour in vain, trying to stabilize the Christmas tree in a standing position. The only words that come out of my mouth are explicit and indelicate. At first, the tree's weight seems manageable; it's not too heavy, but the height of it damns me to failure. There is just simply too much tree and too little of me. The attempts I make to move the tree only get more needles in my hair and I know I'm a fucking mess. When I give up on bringing the tree up to a standing position, I carefully sweep what ornament pieces I can off the floor and trash my pjs in the process.

I sigh, finally giving up, then sit my ass on the side of the couch not occupied by the tree. I take deep calming breaths, attempting to focus on relaxing my mind. And there, at the forethought of my thoughts is Caleb freaking Gardiner.

Isla and Graham always have the best of intentions whenever they offer advice. It's in both of their natures to be generous, but the conversation about Caleb visibly makes me tense and undoes any progress I've made in relaxing. I close my eyes, childishly thinking that if I don't see him, it means I don't have to face him or the budding tension between us.

Right?

Isla has ripped the rug from under me, taking the last of my defenses away. She's told me to act on my feelings for Caleb. But I'm barely coming to terms with the fact that I do find Caleb attractive, or that I'm even interested. The teenage version of Caleb that's always resided in my mind has been ousted by the man I'm becoming reacquainted with.

Unsettled with indecision, I open my eyes, only to behold the chaos in front of me. I've barely made a dent in the cleaning. Graham and Isla are right: I can't do this on my own. Can I swallow my pride and accept Caleb's help? I know in my heart that he is a good man, but I expect mockery and teasing to come hand in hand with his assistance. He was waiting for the tree to fall down to prove his point. I don't think my ego can handle that shit.

I tap my phone open, find Caleb's contact info, and note his personal cell phone number. It hasn't changed in eleven years, and I know in that moment that his steadfast nature is just as much a part of him as is his teasing. I tap on his number, sighing with utter exhaustion.

I haven't made any decisions about where my heart stands now, but I do have to get this mess cleaned up.

My heart sputters as the phone rings.

And rings.

And rings.

caleb

IF YOU NEED ME | JULIA MICHAELS

I t's mid-morning on Friday, and I'm deeply immersed in the process of creating desserts for New Year's Eve. After working through the weekend, I'll present the options to our top investor and Luc, our head chef and owner on Monday.

The current dessert I'm working on is sfogliatella. It's an Italian pastry layered like a croissant but built like a log and filled with ricotta cream. The shape finishes as a lobster's claw and is incredibly labor intensive. With the sort of work I've put into this dessert, I expect Luc will appreciate it. It is after all, the way I caught Luc's attention and got me hired once I graduated. One of my assistant pastry chefs, Evan, is working on the cream filling while James is playing with the pulled sugar designs that will complete the aesthetic for the plate. It'll be finished with a mint gelato that I'll start later tonight.

I spiral the pastry on a rolling pin secured in a bowl so I can pull it out as needed. While I roll the dough into a log, I spread out the thin pastry so I can cover it in butter, which will give it those perfect flaky layers sfogliatella needs. The process takes an endless amount of patience which is what I use to help calm my mind. AirPods in my ears, I'm jamming out to some Bad Religion as I slowly roll the pastry. Evan comes over with a spoonful of the cream. I open my mouth to taste test it, which is nearly perfect.

"Just add a little more lemon," I advise, pulling out my AirPod, then hand him the spoon back. "It should balance out the raspberry. We don't want too sweet."

"You got it boss," Evan salutes me with the spoon and returns to his station.

My phone rings, but I'm covered in butter up to my elbows, and I'm so far in the zone that I wouldn't be able to answer it anyway. I leave my phone out though, just in case. I haven't heard from Rayanne in three days, and I'll admit I'm impressed that the tree has lasted this long in that absurdly small base of hers.

I snort as I recall how utterly ridiculous Rayanne looked. Her hair was an absolute mess, needles stuck throughout her thick white-blonde curls; her tank riding up and her skin sticky from the sap.

She was fucking radiant.

The difference between the way Rayanne looked at me at the beginning of the day to the end when she was yelling at me as I walked out the door almost gave me the confidence to push to test Chris' theory some more. I was so tempted to step back into her apartment and coax a kiss out her, but I didn't want to risk the possibility of her shutting me out. I left with the hope that I could continue to test out Chris' theory in the future.

My phone starts ringing again, and I grin in victory, and I know that it's Rayanne calling me. If my phone is ringing at 11:30 in the morning on a Friday, it is most definitely a tree-related incident. Perhaps that future is sooner than I expected. I continue my steady pace with the sfogliatella.

I'm about halfway through the roll when my phone rings for a third time in twenty minutes. The tree has definitely fallen over. I call out Siri's name from my AirPods telling her to text Rayanne.

"Hey Rayanne," I dictate. "Currently elbow deep in butter for work. I'll call back soon."

Evan and James study me with raised brows of surprise. They're aware of my feelings for Rayanne, so I catch them up on what's going on with her Christmas tree. We discuss the next steps for the sfogliatella and how it might be affected if Rayanne needs me. James offers to make the gelato in case there is a dire emergency.

When the log is finished, and I'm as scrubbed clean as I'll ever be, I step outside into the cool breezy air of a December afternoon. It's chilly enough to need a warm jacket this year, which is a Christmas miracle in itself. It might even be cold enough to get a light dusting of snow if we ever get the clouds of perspiration for it. My mind drifts to kissing Rayanne in the snow, but I push against the daydream.

As much as I enjoy envisioning Rayanne's lips on mine, the truth is that when I started testing out Chris' theory on Tuesday, the results were as effective on me as they were on Rayanne. When I positioned my body in her space and touched her hair as an excuse to feel those thick curls in my fingertips, I felt Rayanne's walls breaking down. I saw—with my own eyes—the moment she started looking at me differ-ent. I don't know if she's aware of the change, but the chem-istry between us has shifted and is now taut with tension. If she had been ready for a kiss, she would have sought it.

No, I don't need to daydream anymore. I just need to see Chris' theory through.

I tap on her name to see what's going on. "Rayanne?" I ask in greeting.

"Caleb? Thank fuck!" The evident relief in her voice raises alarm bells as I receive an invitation for FaceTime and accept it. Rayanne's a fucking mess, one side of her body has her pajamas painted against her body from cleaning up. There's a horizontal tree in the background, and towels are strewn about everywhere, clearly soaked through.

"What happened?" I ask, a smirk escaping unintention-ally. I know what's happened, but I need to hear it from her.

"It was fine," she swears. "For three days, I had it under control." Rayanne sounds cool and appears calm, but it's clear she's struggling with composure. "But I might have filled the tree with too much water last night and I didn't finish all my decorations which are all facing the front door. And... well, it was enough for the tree fell over this morning. It woke me up. The tree, the lights, and candles, it's all covered in water." Her voice raises slightly towards the end, clearly trying to control the panic I know is simmering underneath.

"Fuck," I hiss. "Show me." Any impulse I had for boasting goes out the window when I hear the Christmas lights are covered in water.

Rayanne flips the phone over, and it's as she's described: the tree's weight sags against the floor and the coffee table. The top of the tree is leaning against her couch. She's done some rearranging of the furniture. But there are some delicate ornaments broken into shards that dust the carpet, and some of the candles are tossed carelessly onto the floor. The carpet is covered in towels, but there's clear evidence that she's rotated wet towels to try and catch all the water. She's at risk of some serious water damage if it all doesn't get taken care of.

"Fuck," I exhale through my nose, closely monitoring my own concern. "Ray, are you wearing shoes?"

"Of course, I'm wearing shoes, asshole!" she shouts back, and the panic I've been waiting for shows up finally. "I got my combat boots on." She changes the view camera once more to show me. "See?" She flashes her ruined pajama bottoms with her sturdy combat boots, and I breathe a sigh of relief.

"Of course, you do." I reply, chuckling. Thank fuck for combat boots. "I'll be there soon, okay? I need to wrap up at the restaurant."

"Okay." she smiles. "Oh, Caleb?"

"Yeah?"

"We need towels—lots of them." Rayanne grimaces. "Mine are soaked through and I didn't have many to begin with."

"I'll bring some more over." I grin at her. "See you soon."

I arrive at Rayanne's apartment with my arms full of towels. Before I can knock, the door springs wide open with Rayanne's curse of thanks. The towels I brought block my sight of her. As Rayanne removes them two by two, the disaster of the tree falling comes into view; its troublesome consequences revealed. I silently curse. It's been at least an hour and a half since she called, and who knows how long the tree actually has been on its side.

Rayanne comes back to me bedraggled. She's strategically placed the towels where they're needed for absorbing the most water. She's had a fuck-all morning and I'm ready to offer her a shot when Rayanne hugs me tight around my waist, leaving my shirt wet.

"Thank you." She shudders involuntarily then laughs with relief. I wrap my arms around her neck, welcoming the embrace. Her head fits perfectly against my chest, and I breathe in her scent. There are still hints of honey almond, but it's overpowered by damp pine tree.

"Sorry I'm so late," I mutter into her hair. "I've been working on some ideas for New Year's desserts, and they're labor intensive."

"You're here." she replies, relief etched all through her tone. If I'm not mistaken, she sounds surprised to hear it. I smile, breathing in her damp tree scent, tempted to hold her a little longer and say fuck all to catastrophes. I resist the temptation and pull back, knowing how much work we have ahead of us.

"Come on," I say, dragging myself away. "Let's get the tree back up and rest it against the windows. Then you can take a shower, alright?"

"You're my fucking hero right now, you know that?" Rayanne replies, and I do a double take when she grins up at me through her eyelashes. There's something more than just relief in her expression, and I'm not sure she's aware. It's in her body language and the way that she's been touching me. The shift is so slight, I'm not even sure it's real, but my gut instincts are telling me something about me has changed for her.

Chris' words have echoed in my mind since Tuesday, but today they're hitting me with a full punch in the gut.

This is it.

Today's the day that magic could happen with Rayanne.

84

"You bet your ass I know." I grin down at her. Her blue eyes, wide open with happiness at seeing me, are temptation itself. I temper my impatience down, knowing that this isn't the right time or place. I won't be holding anything back today though, and if she doesn't shy away or flinch at my proximity, then it's game on.

"Come on," I nudge Rayanne to face the catastrophe behind her. "Let's get this fucker standing and get you cleaned up."

"Thank you." Rayanne repeats, breathing out a deep sigh with relief.

"Did you turn into a turntable?" I ask, teasing.

"Oh fuck off," Rayanne says, attempting to shove me away. We carefully work our way back to the tree. On my count, we haul the tree upright, stand still attached at its base.

"Do you want to take the tree out of the base now?" I ask, looking at several possibilities for what we do. The decorations, for all intents and purposes, are a lost cause. Half her ornaments smashed from falling off the tree, and with the lights being immersed in water for an extended period of time, just about everything is going to need to be replaced. If we take the tree out now, it won't be the end of the world, but I can begin cleaning up underneath the tree while it rests. Keeping it in the stand might make it fall over again.

"Won't it need water?" Rayanne asks biting her lip with concern.

"It'll be fine," I reply, trying to assure her. "It takes longer than us being gone for a few hours for it to die."

After a few moments for considering her options, she nods her agreement. "Yeah, alright."

"Hold the tree steady for me again, will you?" Whispers of Tuesday night circle the air as we both remember me testing her limits of my physical proximity in her space. I purposefully put my chin on her thigh. I followed her when she got panicked to see the moment though. Rayanne didn't back away then, nor did she tell me to stop. From what I've seen since I arrived today this, coupled with the fact that she wasn't pushing me away on Tuesday is enough for me to keep pushing the limits.

If Rayanne had been more indulgent, perhaps today would have started differently. My touch lingered on her body more times than I have in my life before. My fingertips tingle to find their place in her curls since I've wanted her for half my life. Instead, I busy my hands by stuffing them into my jean pockets to resist all the temptations that make up Rayanne Miller.

"I got it." She replies, her face surprisingly blank. I take my time moving down to the tree stand, keeping my eyes on Rayanne until I can't anymore. Let her think what she will, but the magic between us is already swirling in the air. *Something* is going to happen today.

We work though quickly because I want her to get warm and dry. Rayanne has been in her wet pajamas for hours. I know she's miserable.

"Go get cleaned up," I urge her on. "I'm sure you want to change." Rayanne studies me for a minute, squinting her eyes at me, unsure of my intentions. I roll my eyes at her, because sometimes she is ridiculously suspicious. "I'm not following you in the bathroom." I wink, just because I love fucking with her. "I have a disaster to clean up, you know."

Rayanne starts to address me with her hands on her hips, as if deliberating her options. Then she huffs and exits the living room, leaving me alone and grinning like an idiot. Whatever was going through her mind must have been a comedy show, because she just blew air at me as a response.

I message Luc, James, and Evan to let them know I'm taking the rest of the day off to assist Rayanne with her emergency. I get Luc's thumbs up and the corners of my lips turn up, thankful that he's a good man and a better chef.

Putting my phone away, I study her living room to decide what to focus on first. The candles and ornaments on the floor gather my attention. I make myself at home searching for her brooms and find them in her utility closet, which is currently empty because of all her towels on the ground. I find a Dutch broom that will collect all the broken shards of ornaments in the carpet and make clean piles. I work my way through the living room, lifting tables, shifting couches, and catching the last of the fuckers who think they can escape me. The damage was worse than I thought. Her towels are completely ruined with shards of ornaments that have become embedded with the water absorbed. I find some trash bags and triple bag them to support the weight of the water and protect against the ornament shards. Looks like we're buying more towels today too.

I repurpose the towels I brought for the spaces that need them the most. When I've finished with the floor, I go back to the tree and assess the lights. Rayanne has sensibly unplugged them. I place the tree against her large bay window to identify what strands of lights are working. Unfortunately, Rayanne doesn't have many that are working consistently. They aren't completely dead, but she needs better ones. And knowing Rayanne's habit of keeping the lights on twenty-four-seven, they'll die before we even get to Christmas day.

Rayanne strides out of her room in an off shoulder green sweater, skinny black jeans, and her combat boots. My breath catches as she marches towards me.

Fuck this shit.

She's so fucking radiant, I'm about to haul her over my shoulders and show her what happens when she exposes her shoulders like that. My imagination teases me with the steps

I'd take, trailing kisses up her neck to that sweet spot behind her ear. I once heard her tell Isla that was her favorite spot to be kissed. I stowed it away alongside the thousands of images, random facts, and preferences that make up Rayanne.

"Hey," I grin, and I don't hide my pleasure at seeing how gorgeous she looks. "Feel better?"

"Positively human." she smiles back. "Thanks for this. You made progress while I was out."

"I did, but you have some casualties, Ray." I reply, furrowing my brows in mock concern.

"What do you mean?!" she asks, instantly worried. The crease between her eyebrows is so fucking cute I want to sweep it clean with kisses.

"Your towels gotta go." I cut to the chase. "Your lights, while they survived for the most part, are old, and I'm pretty sure they won't last the week."

"What do you mean!?" she asks, slightly outraged. "They've lasted me for years."

"Yeah, sweetheart, they're on their last legs." I pronounce dryly. "That's why you need to get new lights."

"Fuck," she breathes out. "I knew the towels were shot, but now the lights too? What about the candles? Are any of them broken?"

"Yeah, Ray, what the hell?" I ask, my curiosity getting the better of me. "Why are the fucking candles on your tree? Isn't that an easy way to burn your apartment down?"

Rayanne laughs, "Not if you let the candles burn for a couple of hours under sharp supervision."

"But…why?"

"There's lots of reasons why," she explains patiently. "But it's a tradition my parents kept while I was growing up, and it's so beautiful that I do it every year."

"Are you sure that's wise?" I ask, raising an eyebrow.

"Yes!" she laughs at me. "Are any of the candles broken?"

"No," I reply with a grunt. "They're fine."

"Good, because this is becoming a really fucking expensive Christmas tree."

"Sorry," I reply, not really feeling sorry at all. I may have hated hauling this tree up to her apartment, but now it gives me the excuse I need to spend time with Rayanne. I have all day to work my way into her heart. Perhaps I'll settle differently in hers by the time we're done today.

"Come on," she says on a sigh. "Let's get this over with."

"I'll drive," I reply. "Anywhere you want to hit up first?" I flash my keys in my palm, ready to go. Rayanne smiles, happy to let me do the honors.

"Breed and Company." she replies, her smile unfurling wider. "They have the best Christmas shit around."

"Which one?" I ask for clarification, as there are at least three locations I know of.

"The one on twenty-ninth, *duh*." she replies, rolling her eyes. "Literally the best and only one in town to go to."

"They *could* have the right tree base size there, since they have a large garden center and all," I tease, lips curling into a smile. "But we might need to hit a Home Depot if they don't have it."

"Honestly, some of their decorations are a little over the top." She replies, "But I like it."

"Their ornaments do remind me of your parents," I say, a smile tugging at the corner of my lips. "Bows... fucking everywhere." I imitate an explosion with my hands and Rayanne giggles. The one time I saw Christmas at Rayanne's parents' house was an event. Big bows, oversized ornaments, fake garlands exploding on every flat surface. It was a fucking Christmas disco in their house. No wonder Rayanne has unrealistic expectations about decorations for her small apartment.

"I don't *have* bows." she concedes stiffly, fighting a smile.

I laugh openly at her, "No you don't, thank god."

"My parents' bows cause nightmares," she replies, shuddering. "Too. Many. Bows."

"And that's why you were going to use one as backup to a star?" I raise an eyebrow. She tries to swat my arm in response, but I dodge her attempt. God, it's so fucking easy to egg her on. She bristles up in defense at my teasing.

"You are such a jerk," Rayanne rolls her eyes at me, finally conceding the point I'm making. "I should have never said that. I fucking *hate* bows."

"So, I was right?" I ask, raising an eyebrow. "You would rather leave your tree bare than put a bow on it?"

At her silent consent, I continue prodding her, knowing I'll get a reaction. "Are you even allowed to sleep during Christmas? Or are your blackout curtains sacrificed to the Christmas Elves because they aren't red, green, or white?"

"Oh, fuck off, Caleb," Rayanne says, as she attempts to punch me. I stop my movement as she skates past me, bursting with laughter. Her loud, carefree laughter bursts from her mouth, and it's so god damned beautiful. It wasn't always so loud in the past. There were years when her brilliance was forcibly dimmed down. Every time I think about it, I'm ready to do the man bodily harm that made Rayanne darken her effervescence. She stands tall now, proud in her body and uninhibited in her joy and feelings. Rayanne finally grasps my arm and offers a short punch as she holds herself steady through her giggles. I press her closer to me, just so I can cherish this moment a little longer.

caleb

HANDS DOWN | DASHBOARD
CONFESSIONAL

I step in my truck as Rayanne hops in, landing with a loud *thwump* on the cushion. The motor comes to life and we're heading down Mopac to Breed and Company. Rayanne's on research mode to tap down mileage for the most efficient itinerary. She's so adorable, casually resting with her boots propped up on my dashboard. Her apparent ease and comfort are such a relief to me that I want to lean in and brush a soft kiss on her forehead. I keep my hands on the wheel and focus on navigating the random pockets of traffic stoppage.

When we arrive at Breed and Company, Rayanne and I

part ways in front of the store. Christmas trees are decorated to greet customers with hundreds of ornaments for sale. Rayanne laughs at the sight before her and begins her search for the new treasures that will come home with her.

I move on to the gardening section searching for lights and tree stands. I wind around until I find the automatic doors and am greeted by a sales associate. When I'm informed that they're out of lights and have the wrong size tree stand, I shift gears and make my way towards the towels. I sort through the different grades of quality of the towels available and try to find something like what she had before. I stack five or six in my arms and make my way back to her.

When I return to the front of the building where I left Rayanne, she's cackling with pleasure as she runs around like a little kid on a treasure hunt for the perfect ornaments, which overflow her basket. I internally cringe because these guys are twenty dollars a pop and she easily has four hundred dollars' worth to sort through. I bite my cheek to contain my entertainment at her wonder in something as trivial as Christmas tree ornaments. I toss the towels on the nearest counter and cross my arms, leaning against a column. Rayanne pauses from her dance of delight to observe the towels by my side with no tree stands or lights in tow.

"No luck?" she asks, a furrow in her brow creases. I resist smoothing it out for her.

"No." I admit. "We're going to need to hit Home Depot for the tree stand."

"Sounds good." Rayanne smiles at me. "Hey, come help me pick out some ornaments because I know you love this shit so much." She points to her overflowing basket.

"I pick this one." I gesture to an over-the-top glittery black and white polka dotted bow right in front of me. It's oversized and could easily take its place at the centerpiece of the tree. "This looks perfect. In fact, I believe this is the bow you wanted on top of your tree."

"You are such an asshole." Rayanne laughs, tugging on my shirt sleeves. "Come *on!* Look at these with me." She attempts to grab my hand to pull me closer, but I'm already looking for the next worst ornament I can find.

"Or what about this?" I hand her an absurdly hideous green, black, red, and white plaid ornament that's thrown up in glitter. "That goes perfect with your décor."

It doesn't. There is nothing about this ornament that goes with her apartment or the aesthetic she's aiming for on Christmas. But it's fucking entertaining to watch her face turn from one of hope to disgust as she looks at my second choice. Like she didn't know I was going to fuck around with her about this. Rayanne tries to hit me again, and I burst with laughter as I dodge her attempts.

"Stop it!" Rayanne hollers when she finally lands a punch on my shoulder. "You are such a jerk!"

"Are you really spending four hundred dollars on ornaments?" I ask, an eyebrow raised. I peruse through the choices given, and they are a little better than the ones I jokingly gave her. She's picked all the ones I would have wanted on my tree if I had to start over again.

"No," she grins, "Just a hundred dollars. These are the best ones I could find. I'm just making myself pick five."

"Then map out a route to the nearest Michaels and we'll get some cheaper ones too." I remind her. "These guys can't be the only ones to decorate that monstrosity." Rayanne glares at me, and I smirk.

"Fine." She concedes as she turns her attention to the ornaments in front of her.

Of the twenty assorted ornaments Rayanne has chosen, we have a hell of a time picking the right ones for the tree. There are ten that she can't decide between, and at the end of the tireless debate, she picks the five random ones from the mix. Rayanne's equally pleased and annoyed because she's limited herself to five, when she really wants ten. She packs up the towels I picked out for her, places the ornaments in her basket, and a few random knickknacks she's found in the home center, then looks at me expectantly.

"Go on," I nudge her. "I'll be there in a minute. I need to check on something right quick." Rayanne gives me a dubious brow then walks away when I keep nudging her out the door. I grab the other ornaments that made her top ten and throw in the ostentatious black and white bow for good measure. I wander towards the garden center where I find the associate who helped me before.

"Are you sure she's just your friend?" the saleswoman asks suspiciously. "When you asked about the Christmas tree lights and the stand, you told me—"

"I'm working on it," I wink at her. "I'm hoping this will help." I put the ornaments down on the register and she grins at me.

"Um, yeah, that might do it," she replies, quickly assessing all the ornaments. "Oooh! These are such good choices—and *expensive*. I saw her go crazy shopping for them. I think they might help." She rambles happily as she rings up my ornaments, then wraps them up individually.

"They were her favorites," I shrug. "Besides, she has a nine-and-a-half-foot tree and it's just too big for five ornaments. It'll be what she wants."

The associate grins back at me. "How can she say no when you offer her a gift like this?"

"I hope so," I reply, running a hand through my hair. I tap my phone for payment as directed. All the ornaments are gathered in a Breed & Co bag, which she hands me as the payment is completed.

"It's a sweet gesture," she smiles at me and hands over the bag of ornaments. "Good luck!"

"Thanks, happy holidays!" I wave goodbye and head out to find Rayanne.

Rayanne points to the truck, then throws her arms up in a *what gives* gesture. I shrug, beep the truck open for her, and step into it. "Seriously though!?" she asks while hopping into the truck. "What took so long?"

I show her the bag of ornaments. "You are not allowed to open this until we get to your apartment."

"Color me intrigued." Rayanne tilts her head in a questioning gesture, then attempts to peek through the top. I playfully swat her creeping hand away from the bag.

"Good," I grin mischievously at her. I plop them down and start the truck. "Stay intrigued, and don't try that again."

The rest of the afternoon passes amicably. We've completed our mission at Michaels for new lights and cheaper ornaments and we even found the right size tree stand. Each moment with her gives me an opportunity to learn more of her quirks, what she loves and dislikes. I find new ways to make her laugh like she hasn't in years. I soak up my time with her like it's the last chance I'll have alone with her. Because as far as I'm concerned, it is.

If I thought I liked Rayanne in my head or the girl I grew up idolizing, they are nothing compared to the woman she's become. She's incredibly funny, smart, and quick on her feet. She doesn't take my shit and hands it back to me when I'm being an asshole—which I am on a regular basis. I see the interest in Rayanne's eyes and the way she casually touches me. I see her ease with me in the way she props her feet on my dashboard while we drive around town. I feel our friendship strengthen when I test her boundaries, and she laughs her way through. I test myself, pushing my own limits because the more time I spend with her, the more I want her alone.

We unanimously decide to grab some fries and shakes for appetizers from P.Terry's before heading over to Central Market to pick out food for dinner. Rayanne checks my theory on opening the bag of ornaments several times, then laughs at me and the way I smack her hands out of the way each time. The potential in friendship and love that I've always believed in is evident between us. Is it the magic between us, or just a series of circumstances that allow me this small gift?

As I move on to the dinner prep, Rayanne pours herself a glass of wine and props herself across the island. We're taking a well-earned break from Christmas cleaning and managed to control the worst of the damage. Rayanne wanted a stir fry for dinner and insisted on both tofu and chicken for protein. While they marinate, I prep the veggies.

"Would you stop!" I ask, flicking water from my glass at Rayanne. She squeals with laughter, dodging my assault of water droplets. This is the third or fourth time Rayanne has attempted to help around the kitchen, but she's distracting me. "Sit your ass down and relax, alright? I got this."

"But—" Rayanne pouts, and it's the cutest frown I've ever seen.

"Seriously," I emphasize, pausing my veggie prep. I grin at her, motioning her to put her sweet ass down in the chair in front of me. Has she never had anyone cook for her before? I focus on my task at hand. "Drink that glass of wine while I cook. You've had a long day, and you've earned a break."

"Fine." Rayanne huffs out her resignation. She seats herself in front of the hummus and veggies I organized for appetizers and takes a long sip of her wine. Her shoulders sag with relaxation, and she smiles happily at me. "You want a glass?"

"Not now," I reply, shifting the carrots over to the side and begin on cleaning the snap peas. "I'll take one during dinner though."

"Okay," Rayanne says, swiping a carrot from the veggie pile for the stir fry. I'd smack her hand away but am secretly pleased to see her move across the island as she attempts to steal the food for our meal. It's the sort of small gesture of intimacy that reassures me of her comfort with me. I'm unable to express what it means to me to see how much she's opened up. Rayanne dips the carrot into the hummus and munches on it. A small smile tugs at her lips while she watches me cook, and it almost feels like she approves of the effortless ease between us while I prep.

"How's head-pastry-chefing at *Les Portes du Plaisir* coming along?" she asks, being ridiculous and exaggerating the French name.

I snort at her description of my job. "It's fine." I reply. "Getting ready for the New Year's Eve special."

"What does that mean?" she asks, tracing the edge of her wine glass with her fingertips. I don't think she's flirting with me on purpose, but the look she gives me through her lashes test all of my patience. Rayanne Miller is completely oblivious to the kind of impact she has on me. A deep sweep of her eyelashes, a small curve turns up on her lips, and then Rayanne looks down at her glass of wine…almost shyly.

Does she know?!

If that's the fucking case, she'll be begging me to stop giving her all the attention she deserves.

"Well," I begin, finishing the snap peas to focus on my composure. It's not much time because cutting them up takes me all of fifteen seconds. I start on the bell peppers and check the rice. "We're working on finding the right pastry to serve as an exclusive for the New Year."

"Did you find it yet?" She asks, taking a sip of wine.

"I think so," I reply. "It's labor intensive, so the love and time it takes to make it checks all the boxes for the special feature for this time of year. If I had to do it every week, I'd never have a day off."

"What is it?" she asks.

"Sfogliatella," I answer, finishing off the veggies.

"I haven't heard of it." Rayanne answers. "What kind of pastry is it?"

"It's an Italian pastry layered like a croissant," I begin, giving the simplified explanation. "But it's first rolled out like a log and then shaped to create a lobster's claw and has a ricotta cream filling."

"It sounds delicious!" she beams at me. "I know croissants take a lot of folding—is it like that?"

"Yeah," I grin, pointing at her. "But I'm not sure you want to know about how much work it takes."

"Probably not," she laughs. "Then tell me how you're changing the traditional recipe. Because knowing you, there's some sort of modification."

"It'll have a lemon-raspberry crème filling with a mint gelato," I reveal, and her eyes open wide. "And the sfogliatella itself is bite size with a raspberry-mint compote drizzled on the top." The only people that know the full extent of details for the dessert are Evan and James. Luc trusts me on this task, even if I'm preparing other options for Monday's tasting.

"That sounds amazing," Rayanne whispers.

"It should be." I answer, winking. "But I haven't finished the sfogliatella shell yet. It needs to rest today and then I'll finish preparing the filling and bake everything on Sunday."

An excuse begins to form in my mind so I can see Rayanne later this weekend.

"Grab the chicken and tofu, will you?" I change the subject. Any awkwardness between us is long gone, and all that remains is the raw chemistry that makes us work so well together. It's so effortless to be with Rayanne. Today has been a testimony to what I always knew is between us. I want to make a move, but Rayanne hasn't given me any indications that it's what she wants.

So, I wait.

Rayanne eagerly jumps off the chair to be helpful and I find myself watching her move. I get lost in the distraction of how closely those jeans hug her ass. I study her body for imperfections that I know aren't there, just to observe the sway of her hips.

"Should I drain the meat out of the marinade?" she asks.

"Nope," I reply. "Just leave it here, but get a small saucepan, will you? I'm going to thicken up some of this marinade as a sauce." I turn off the rice to let it rest as I prepare a pan to sear the protein. I start breading the tofu then take the chicken thighs and plate them as well. Rayanne watches me dance around her kitchen. I catch her eye, and that small smile she offers me only encourages me to test our boundaries more. If I get to kiss Rayanne tonight, it'll be a fucking marvel when I do.

"Did you always like cooking?" Rayanne asks, as I keep moving through her kitchen. I grab the third pan that barely fits her stovetop for the veggies. I begin sautéing the broccoli, baby corn, water chestnuts, and carrots. I place the tofu and chicken on the pan side by side and let the tofu fry in the oil as I shift the chicken around. I pour the marinade into the saucepan and put it on high for boiling.

"Yeah, I love it." I reply, a big grin unfurling. "Mom

taught me well. Isla and I had some good times with her in the kitchen."

"Isla has told me about some of the cooking nightmares, too." Rayanne smirks, like she's getting away with a dig at me.

"Just in the beginning!" I reply, flicking some water once more. Rayanne squeals when she dodges the wrong way, and the water droplets come into contact with her face. "I became good at setting up for meals, and then when I out prepped everyone in the kitchen, Mom began showing me more complicated tasks in the kitchen."

"I noticed." Rayanne grins, wiping her face. "A girl could get used to this, you know, having dinner prepared for her every night."

"All you have to do is ask." I give her a teasing grin, and she blushes. Rayanne knows it's true. There's a moment of truth between us as we gaze at each other. I'd do anything for her. Now that we are learning more about each other as adults, the honest devotion I have always felt for her has only intensified. Rayanne blushes again, shifting her body closer to mine. I don't miss the change of posture. Had I not been in the middle of cooking dinner, I would have taken steps to be closer to her too.

As the marinade boils, I shake up the protein and check the bottoms of the tofu. I flip them over and shake the pan again, then season the veggies, and begin layering in the peppers and mushrooms. I check the rice and begin fluffing it out with a wooden spoon.

"Better get the bowls ready and bring them over here." I notify her. "Dinner's going to be ready in a couple of minutes."

While Rayanne sets the table, I finish up sautéing the protein and rotating the tofu on the side so that it gets crispy. I test out the marinade, place some thickener in it and continue to cook it down.

"Do you cook at home a lot?" Rayanne asks.

"Yeah." I reply. "I might as well. There isn't anyone that's going to do a better job than I am, except Luc."

"He *is* the head chef." Rayanne counters, a small smile revealing her entertainment. "You'd think he'd have some talent in the kitchen."

"A bit." I wink at her. When I've determined the marinade has turned into the perfect glaze, I plate everything in the bowl. Rayanne pours me a glass of wine. The dining table isn't big, so we sit side by side. The wine is excellent, my woman is beautiful, and the food is good.

"Shut the fuck up, Caleb!" Rayanne shouts, mouth full of food. She finishes her first bite then braces herself against the table. "Holy crap! This is so good!"

I laugh, "Glad you like it."

"Are you kidding?" she rolls her eyes in delight. "Why aren't you the sous chef?"

"Because I love baking." I reply simply. "I find the method and order in complex pastries. And it's a soothing process."

"Which is needed," Rayanne completes the unsaid statement I don't say aloud.

"What did Isla tell you?" I ask, cautiously. It's true, that I find a steady peace while I work. I just didn't know that Isla shared that particular detail with anyone.

"Just enough that I know it's helpful for finding inner peace." She replies. Rayanne takes a moment to study me, then offers a comforting smile.

"Yeah," I reply, digging into my food. "It does a pretty good job."

But I don't need it when I'm with you.

The words are dying to escape, so I take a sip of wine instead. The clean citrus from the marinade pairs nicely with the fruity front of the Sancerre. When I look back at Rayanne, it's like she knows my mind. She places her small, delicate fingers on mine. Unable to resist, I kiss the underside of her wrist lightly. The scent of her honey almond fragrance is there. I tuck her hand into her side before I'm tempted to do more. Rayanne offers a light squeeze of my fingers. She's accepted the attention I've given her today. It's a double-edged sword, stirring up my feelings for her while I try not to overwhelm her with my affection.

"Thanks," I say, softly. "Today's been great."

"Yeah, it has." Rayanne replies, slightly breathless. Her gaze lingers on me as I look down at her. There's an opportunity to press my lips on hers if I want, but my instincts tell me to wait. Wait for Rayanne to tell me that she wants me to kiss her. And I will, so I dig into the rice and bide my time for her permission.

Dinner is companionable as Rayanne tells me about launching her marketing consultation business she's trying to establish for herself. She's in her element discussing the vision she has for all that she can offer startup companies and the goals for her career. She's so fucking brilliant that it's scary. I promise her that I'll keep my ear to the ground for opportunities that might interest her. Maybe *Les Portes du Plaisir* can help launch her consultation business when the time is right.

When we finish dinner, Rayanne stands to take our bowls back to the sink. I stop her before she can move too far away and wrap my arms around her waist. She puts the bowls on the table and hugs me back. Knowing her mind and spending the day with her has only increased my need for her touch. I've resisted Rayanne long enough today, and now I just simply want to hold her. I graze my lips over her stomach so lightly, I don't even know if she feels it because my arms are wrapped around her so tightly. She hugs me back just as fiercely. Rayanne has felt the shift between us, and to feel her embrace me just as tightly is a balm to my senses.

"Caleb." Rayanne breathes out my name on a sigh. "Talk to me. What is this for?"

"You give me strength," I murmur. "I just need some more."

"Oh Caleb," she sighs as she runs her fingers through my hair. I hum in pleasure and this time kiss her under her bra line. Rayanne protests weakly and I back off. I have to fucking kiss her properly first before I start anything like that. I reluctantly let go, grab our dishes, and take them to the sink.

"Go look in the bag now." I change the subject, worrying I overdid it. Rayanne remains frozen in place, clearly reacting to my selfish moment of indulgence when I kissed her intimately. Clearly, she didn't miss that small indiscretion. Is she okay? Perhaps I overstepped the fragile boundary between us.

"Ray?" I ask, trying to grab her attention once more. "Are you okay?" She blinks slowly at me as if she doesn't see me. Suddenly, she stands taller, as if her mind has been made up with a decision. I watch her tentatively, worried she's about to kick me out.

"Ray?" I ask, one more time. This time she looks up with recognition. "Go look in the bag." I repeat, smiling.

"I can look!?" Rayanne asks blinking, and I notice she's back to normal. Excitement flashes in her eyes as she grins at me. Whatever that moment was, it's over now. I exhale, relieved that I didn't push my luck.

"Yeah, go grab it," I urge her on. She smiles as she walks past me searching for the bag of ornaments. Rayanne locates it on the couch in the living room, skipping to it like a kid with all eagerness and anticipation.

I stop doing the dishes to watch her open the bag. Rayanne laughs with delight, then unpacks one of the ornaments that she debated on so heavily. She looks back up at me, slack-jawed with wonder.

"Are you fucking serious right now?"

I shrug. "You have a big ass tree and five ornaments weren't enough."

Rayanne charges back to me, bag in tow, and gives me another bear hug. As tiny as she is, and as much as I tower over her, she's the one making me feel breathless. "Thank you." she says, voice muffled in my chest. "They're perfect."

"Did you find my extra one?"

"What?" She looks up, completely confused.

"Search again."

Because clearly, she didn't find the bow ornament. I brace myself for the punch coming. This time, when she opens the bag up to discover the ostentatious bow tie, she throws paper at me. I laugh at her as she attempts to cover me in tissue paper.

"It should be perfect: front and center." I grin helplessly. "About, ye high?" I position my hand two feet taller than myself, clearly positioning for the bow ornament to hold the place of honor.

"You jerk." She punches my stomach, and I chuckle. It doesn't hurt.

"You fucking love it." I laugh at her again. "And no take backsies on a gift." I interrupt her as she opens her mouth in protest. I laugh as I wrap my arms around her so she can't escape. I lower my chin to the crook of her neck. I breathe in her honey almond scent and sigh happily.

"That one's a gift." I speak against her heated skin, "The rest are just to fill up that ridiculous tree."

"Fine," she huffs out a laugh and steps away from me. Rayanne knows that I've invoked one of her girl code rules against her. "Take a break from the dishes and help me with this tree." She moves through the living room, swiping and tapping at her phone. Christmas music begins playing from the speaker as a smile quirks from the corner of my mouth. Rayanne instructs Alexa to play her Christmas Spotify list, then inspects the tree that's leaning against her window.

As we rearrange furniture, put the tree back in the stand, and arrange the ornaments in groups, I'm waiting for the magic's blessing to indicate the right time to kiss my sister's best friend. My impatience grows bold, always seeking the right moment to take the next step that has always felt like natural progression to me. I shamelessly touch her as much as I think I can get away with. When I look at Rayanne and see how comfortable she is with my brazen intimacy, she doesn't hide or shy away. She accepts my attention and doesn't back away from our physical closeness. Rayanne seems to want me as much as I want her, which is the only encouragement I need to keep it up.

We fall effortlessly into a routine, singing along with her Spotify list while we string the new lights on her tree. I take the lead in placing the lights strategically on bottom and work my way up to the top. Rayanne follows me and adjusts the lights to her own vision of what she wants the lights to look like.

The music is the last piece of the puzzle needed to complete the magic. We rediscover how well we sing together while laughing with and at each other. We sing over-dramatically while placing the ornaments around the tree. The light in her eyes is captivating. I've never spent this much time with her while she's happy.

While I'm up on the ladder, I place the bow ornament front and center as the first one on the tree. Rayanne hands me the ornaments she wants on the top then place them strategically at her request. When she squeals in delight with her vision coming to life, it is the final moment to embolden me. Rayanne looks at me with such deep affection that I know that the magic in the room isn't just one-sided. Rayanne feels it as much as I do.

I climb down slowly, facing Rayanne, unable to break eye contact from her. Rayanne's smile is slow and sensual, but I stop at the ladder's edge when I reach it. My body tenses with the need to close the gap that would lead to a kiss. But I pause for her consent, waiting for Rayanne's decision. She takes a couple of steps forward, pauses, then looks down at her feet, clearly considering. Her eyes are wide, clear, and vulnerable as they look into mine. Rayanne wants me enough that I consider closing the space between us. When she bites her lip and looks up at me, it's the encouragement I need to take those final steps towards her, observing how bright the light in her eyes shine.

"Rayanne?" I ask, brushing a curly lock from her face. She leans into the touch and my heart soars. *This is happening.* It's really, honest to god, happening.

"Yeah?" Rayanne leans in, removing any of the space between us.

I can't ask the question I'm dying to say aloud. My heart is so full of anticipation, I feel like I might throw up. We both know where I stand, which is at her side. I'd do anything for her, but I need her to make the next move and tell me that this is what she wants.

"Is it okay if I try something?" Rayanne whispers. I feel her body brush against mine as she moves to stand on her tippy toes.

"You can try anything you like," I offer graciously, a small smile unfurling.

"Good," Rayanne purrs as she brushes my hair from my face. She runs her fingers through my hair, and I reflexively curl my arms around her waist. We both know this embrace is new and full of intention. I'm so worried she's changed her mind, but she presses her body into mine as she leans up to place her hands on either side of my face. "When did you become so handsome, Caleb Gardiner?" Rayanne whispers. "When did this…"

She interrupts herself, her fingers tracing down my temple and to my cheekbones. Her touch scorches my skin, and I'm ready to burst from the steady pace of her exploration.

"Ray," I warn. I can't help it, if she doesn't make up her mind soon, I'm doing it for the both of us.

"Sweetheart," she whispers, testing the word out. It's a balm to my ears and soothes my soul. It's the permission I've been dying to have to make my move. I lean down and lightly touch my lips to hers. It's soft, inviting, and gentle. I'm not about to scare the woman of my dreams off—not when she finally seems so present and willing to try something new. The kiss she offers in return is also light, but she presses firmly. Rayanne tightens her grip in my hair, then tugs as she opens her mouth invitingly. I skim my tongue across her lower lip. At her gasp, I slip it into her mouth and feel the movement of her tongue catch mine. They dance and Rayanne nips at my bottom lip. I growl with pleasure as she tugs on my hair again. I pull her closer into my embrace, kissing her with the passion that's built up for the last twelve years.

I was right. Kissing Rayanne Miller is the embodiment of perfection. Her lips and tongue are made for mine. Her body pressed against me feels like it's shaped to mold itself with mine. It's just the two of us in the moment: Rayanne and Caleb, a man and a woman kissing as if their lives depended on each other for their happiness. She softens as I deepen the kiss. When she wraps her arms around my neck, I hike her legs up around my waist and let her feel the impact of how she affects me. Rayanne pulls back, slightly breathless from our embrace. Her delicate fingertips lightly touch my cheekbones as I adjust my grip to hold her tighter.

The questions in her eyes pull her away, and the moment between us is lost as she slides down my body when I let her go. I can see it plainly on her face: the consequences of our kissing are taking over whatever impulsive desire she feels for me in the moment. The look of joy in her eyes turns to all scrutiny and concern. She might have given me permission to kiss her, but the minute I deepen the moment, I lost her. Rayanne clearly isn't ready, and all the hope that swelled within me is turning into heavy lead in my stomach.

"Ray?" I ask, hoping that the question doesn't sound pleading. *This is good. This is good, Ray, don't pull back.*

"Oh Caleb," she sighs, unable to look at me. She steps back, so that there's at least two or three feet separating us. "I think you should go."

I want to argue with her, to tell her *we* were always meant to happen. That chemistry which swirls between us is the same magic I've always felt beside her. It's the same magnetic pull that always brings us back together. We have always been this good. I just needed her to *recognize* it. I want her to embrace what's right in front of her.

Take it, Ray. Pick me.

"This was always right, sweetheart," I sigh, desperate to contain my feelings. Rayanne's eyes have widened at the term. It cuts like a double-edged sword between us. "What we share—this magic—it isn't just a moment. We're *real* together. You and—"

"Caleb," Rayanne cuts me off, lifting her hand in a stopping motion to seize my words. She stands tall and rigid like an oak tree, clearly troubled and uncomfortable. "Not now, I just… I need time. I don't know what to think right now."

"Is it Isla?" I ask, unwilling to give this up. "Because—"

"No, Caleb." She shuts her eyes with frustration. "For once, it's not Isla. I don't know where to go from this—"

"Forward is generally the right motion," I intone dryly,

unable to help myself. "We can't take that back, and even if we could, I wouldn't."

"No, I don't suppose you would," Rayanne snaps, and I know I've gone too far. My heartstrings pull, and even though I know I'm the cause of her frustration, I want to fix everything and make it better. The only move right now is to let Rayanne be. I gather my things, keeping my eyes on her while I can. I feel the heat of her gaze on mine. When I look back at Rayanne, I feel the trouble and conflict building within her.

Can I fix this? I ask, pleading with my eyes. Rayanne shakes her head no.

Go, she tells me silently.

"Alright," I begin, leaning down to kiss her on the forehead quickly. I can't help it. Even as I look down at her, Rayanne's eyes are shut, but she leans into the embrace. Whatever she's fighting inside, she still feels the attraction between us. I sweep her hair back from her face just to get a clear look at her. If I see her eyes, maybe I'll understand better. If I can sense her hesitations, then I can fix it. But as I search, she refuses to make eye contact, and the immediate solution I need isn't there. Alright then, I'll give Rayanne the space she needs. "I'm going. Keep the ladder, and I'll come back Sunday to pick it up."

Rayanne nods, her eyes slightly widened with vulnerability, but her body's tensed with discomfort. I let go at the thought of my touch making her uncomfortable. I don't quite understand what's happening in Rayanne's mind, but I understand that the acknowledging the shift in our relationship is a lot to process. The intensity of our chemistry is hard for Rayanne to adjust to, and she just needs the space to process her own feelings so she can make her own choices in her own time.

I pick up the trash beside her door because it will take me

one stop versus three for her. Keys in hand with trash in the other, I head out of her apartment. An idea that trickled into my mind as we made dinner begins to blossom in my mind as a full scheme. While I'm technically coming back for my ladder, I'm also bringing her something as well.

A dessert, I think, in the shape of a lobster's claw.

rayanne

IT WAS ALWAYS YOU | MAROON 5

The wonder of a Texas sunset fills the sky with dusky blues, pinks, red, and orange which contrast against the purple-lined clouds. Its beauty eases my mind as I close my eyes and breathe in the cool evening air. The sounds of traffic slowly disappear as I inhale and exhale. I breathe into the stillness and release any concerns that fill my mind.

I'm out on my balcony meditating because it's the next best thing to finding Caleb Gardiner in Austin, Texas and throttling him—or kissing him senseless. I'm not sure what I want to do. I inhale slowly, trying to focus on what I've learned about meditation and the practices needed to achieve inner tranquility. I focus on the details of the wind blowing, the muted traffic, and the beats of my heart. I exhale the pressure point of Caleb out of my body, and breathe in slowly, focusing on the stillness of my mind.

Caleb steps off the ladder, gazing at me with such affection that I know I'm the continuing exhale to his inhale. He wants me so badly, but he holds back his desire. It's his restraint coupled with his patience and that devious sex hair that makes me want to cave. A slight upturn on his lips, like he knows which secret I want to be told. I want to feel his lips on mine. I brush his hair out of his face, marveling at how soft and thick it is. I get lost in the closed space between us and touch his beautiful, chiseled cheekbones and drop the mask.

I tell him *yes*.

I give myself the permission to take what I want.

I expected a deep, fervent kiss, filled with the intensity I see in Caleb's eyes, but he drops such a featherlight touch on my lips that I yearn to explore it further. I press my lips firmly against his and the passion that's been stirring inside me bursts as his tongue traces my bottom lip. It's an invitation to deepen the kiss—and god, I've never craved such an invitation before. The press of his body and his firm lines fit my soft curves perfectly. I melt into his arms as our tongues dance. It's such a perfect combination of exploration and passion that I lift my arms around his neck and Caleb hikes my legs around his waist, pulling me in tight and close. I inhale his scent then exhale the warmth of his body around mine, knowing I found the peace I've sought today.

Fuck.

I open my eyes with my surroundings encompassing me. Traffic blares in my ears, the sunset has dimmed, and Caleb Gardiner is still the center of my tranquility. It's been two days, and everything in my apartment has his touch on it. The floor is immaculate, the hallway is trash free, and the refrigerator is full of his stir fry because he left me enough food for a week. A part of me has gotten used to the small changes of cleanliness in my apartment and seeing his presence everywhere I look. But it's still very overwhelming, and I don't know how to process the potent presence of Caleb Gardiner in my space.

Excising Caleb from my mind and apartment is a lost cause. His presence is unrelenting, and I'm managing it all by doing things like meditating. I sigh as I pick up the yoga mat from my balcony and head back inside to my apartment. The ladder says hello from the wall, only to remind me of that beautiful, magical day that led to our first kiss.

I knew I liked Caleb. Growing up with him on either side of Isla or me, kept us entertained with his humor and sarcasm. The way we gave each other shit then made each other laugh lay in the foundation of our chemistry. It's easy to be around him, partly because he's always been there. As we spent more time together on Friday, I was reminded that being with Caleb is just another extension of myself. If Isla has always known my mind, Caleb has always known my heart.

I know what draws me to him; I know the reasons why I feel so attracted to Caleb. He surprised me in so many ways on Friday that I'm relearning who Caleb is to me now. I've felt the magic stir between us throughout the week. When he insisted I take a shower and allow the time needed for myself, I let the rest of my guard down, understanding that he felt more compassion than spite. Then he insisted I sit and relax while he made dinner. The small details of the day flash before my eyes: Caleb dancing around me in Breed and Company, taunting me with ugly ornaments. Caleb and his smiles made just for me in his truck. The way he always opened the door for me and smacked my hands away from the bag that revealed all the extra ornaments he bought for me.

It's apparent now, but I understand that I was always the central weight to his gravity. Perhaps I should be ashamed of taking advantage of his affection for me, but I just *really* needed it then. He offered his affection with no expectations, and damn him for it, because it was exactly what I needed.

I didn't expect the shift of my attraction to change so fast. I couldn't foresee the magnetic pull to Caleb and how it would weave into my heart and soul as he took care of me that day. I didn't expect my lips would brush against his. The transition from family friend to something more is so effortlessly easy. I keep reeling from my reactions to him and how I could just be myself with him all day. My heart grew three sizes bigger as I kept anticipating this disaster to be thrown back in my face only to find him tending to me and this gigantic mess I made.

When Caleb hugged me like his life depended on it, then kissed me beneath my breastbone, I forgave him because I felt the desperate need for his touch and our physical connection. But somehow, my logic became twisted as he lifted me in his arms and wrapped my legs around his waist. My mind shut down. *I* shut down, not trusting the desire that escalated so quickly.

I want him.

Badly.

I could never have imagined how perfect it would feel to have our tongues dance, nor could I have anticipated that the press of our bodies would feel like arriving home from a long day of work.

I should have seen it coming. I should have prepared myself for his persuasive lips to coax mine open. I should have been ready to turn down his irresistible mouth, and that magical tongue of his working expertly against mine. I should have been able to restrain my arms as they wrapped around his neck to pull him closer.

But with Isla demanding that I put my happiness first, I stopped fighting it. And Caleb…I stopped resisting the happiness I found with him. When I accepted his lips against mine, I chose selfishness. And now I don't know if I want to take what I want, because all I can see at the end of the day is pure joy. I don't know if my heart is ready for such pure, unadulterated happiness.

I don't know if I can do this with Caleb. I don't know if I can live with that urgent need that propels me towards unequivocally changing our relationship. Until this week, Caleb has always been Isla's little brother. *Always.* But this week is catching up with me and I'm on sensory overload as I'm spending time with the man Caleb is today. It's just too much, too fast.

Caleb's attention to detail, the way he always put me first, and the way his eyes watch me as I move—it's fucking intoxicating. He courts me with a full court press, expecting a win at the end I can't promise. The worst part is that I know all of this is a shadow of how he would care for me. The focus and attention that Caleb would offer for my attention is the most exhilarating *yes* I've ever wanted to give into.

I've spent the last three years recovering from a relationship that required demanding therapy, self-evaluation, and patience for accepting who I am and what I need. My ex demanded my body, soul, and mind at any given time, and he still haunts me—whether I want him to or not. I can say with full confidence now that I've done everything I can to recover from his abandonment of me. With all the suffering I've endured, I can admit that I'm now a better woman because of it. But that doesn't mean I'm ready for a new relationship and what Caleb wants from me are promises I can't keep at the end of the day.

I need to talk to Isla again. I need her to help me process all the feelings swirling inside of me. I want to understand *why* exactly she's okay with the idea of Caleb and me being together. Because as tempting as this potential relationship with Caleb is, what happens if we fall apart and break up? Say shit hits the fan and we can't fix what's broken—then I've lost the two most important people in my life. I honestly don't understand how she could be okay with this outcome. It's also really fucking weird that the only person I can talk about this with is my best friend and Caleb's sister.

I take a moment to consider everything Caleb and I still have to discuss. I need to woman up and face the storm of feelings stirring inside me. I glance back at the ladder that's been prone on my wall since we finished decorating. I reluctantly pull out my phone and deliberate on calling Caleb.

My phone buzzes, and I stare blankly at it, not computing that it is in fact, Caleb, calling me.

Weird...

"Caleb." I manifest confidence, even though it's a struggle. The only reason I kicked him out of my apartment was because my need for him shocked me so greatly that I needed him to leave. I felt bad demanding his departure, but at the time, I was unable to comprehend all my feelings for Caleb.

"Hey." Caleb says, and he sounds like himself. Why isn't he mad at me for making him leave on Friday night? The ease of his baritone makes me squeeze my thighs together. I'm utterly frustrated at his casual tone and insanely furious at myself for reacting to his voice.

"Hi." I squeak.

So much for manifesting confidence.

"So, I need to pick up my ladder." Caleb says. "Is it okay if I swing by?"

I breathe a sigh of relief, "Yeah, that's perfect."

Perhaps we can talk this out when he gets here, and I'll have a better idea of what it is that I want.

"I'm on my way then." he replies. "I'm coming from the restaurant."

"How far out are you?"

"Fifteen minutes," he says. "Is that okay? You want coffee or anything?"

"Sure, that'd be great."

I just need more time to consider what it is that I want.

"Peppermint Mocha from Starbucks?" Caleb asks.

I reflexively pull my phone from my ear and glare at him like he can see my surprise. How the fuck does he know that? That's been my go-to drink for years. The fact that he knows my favorite coffee order sends me reeling. Who pays attention to such small things like coffee orders?

"Um, yeah, that's perfect." I pause, sounding ridiculous. "Thanks. How did you—"

"I wasn't blind every time we shopped with Isla during Christmas." Caleb interrupts. "It's not difficult to pay attention to something like a coffee order, Rayanne."

"But—" I pause again. I pull my phone away from my ear and stare at it like I can see his reaction through it. When was the last time Caleb and I went shopping with Isla?

"Fuck, Caleb, that was like, last year during Christmas."

"It's coffee, Rayanne," he replies, and I hear the shrug in his voice. "See you in half an hour."

"See you," I reply, breathless when I consider his timing. I have half an hour before Caleb gets here. I look around trying to find messes I need to clean up, but the apartment is perfect. I spot a few dishes that need tending to and take care of them, then run into the bathroom.

I stare at myself in the mirror. It's only six o'clock in the evening, but I'm still in my workout pants and wearing one of the baggy shirts that I sleep in. Men don't see me dressed like this. I start perusing my closet for the right outfit, trying not to panic because I'm acting like I do when I like someone. I'm falling into old habits for Caleb and the fact that I'm behaving this way makes me want to spiral. I pause, take a steadying breath, and breathe through it.

I can do this. I can find an outfit that works.

I finally pull out my distressed light wash jeans. I know my ass looks good in them, but they're casual enough that I wouldn't wear them for a date. I run my fingers through my collection of shirts, waiting to feel the right material. It's a cool, light cotton rayon combo. The jungle green top makes me smile; the square neckline is open and sexy, and the shirt hugs my curves. I don't feel like I'm dressing up for Caleb with this outfit; I feel like myself.

As I undress, the sight of my neon pink Victoria's Secret bra makes me scoff, then I snort with humor. It's completely useless for support as it's fully stretched out. It really should have been tossed in the trash two years ago. It's comfortable though, and I only wear it in my apartment. Isla would kill me if she knew I still had it. But knowing Caleb as I do, he might say something to Isla, just to tease me. For the sake of my stretched-out Victoria's Secret bra, I change into something new that Isla might approve of. I try not to pay attention to the fact that this is for Isla's younger brother.

I pull out a new white unlined lace balconette that Isla gave me recently. I test it with the shirt on and am pleased with the results. I don't look like I'm trying with a push up, and there's enough to suggest cleavage, but not offered on a platter. I take one last glance at my reflection in the bathroom mirror to determine if I look acceptable.

As I walk out of my closet, I catch a glimpse of my hair and groan at how limp it looks. I pull out my hair dryer to blow it out to my satisfaction. When I finish, it looks normal.

I sigh, looking at the unattractive dark circles under my eyes.

I need concealer.

A knock comes from the entry which makes me jump. Caleb is here, and I've run out of time.

I run over to the door and he's there: coffee in one hand, a small cooler in the other. Caleb is still wearing his chef's jacket all buttoned up. His hair expertly falls in his face, elevating his looks to full level sex god status. I feel myself gaping at him, completely forgetting my manners. The killer combo of hair, chef's jacket, and my favorite coffee order has me eye-fucking him.

God damnit. Did he plan this? I'm practically panting and he's only at the door, waiting for me to let him in.

"Here." I begin, belatedly. "Come in." I'm reeling from the intensity of my reaction to him. Apparently two days is too long without him. And as reluctant as I am to admit it, I missed the fuck out of Caleb.

He's made a hard week so easy, and he understands me so well. The fight against him has been difficult, and now that he's here in front of me, all I want to do is to drink him in.

He grins, "Thanks. This is for you." He offers my coffee which I take gratefully. I exhale a breath, offer him a small smile and take a sip of my coffee. It's the perfect temperature. The taste of the chocolatey peppermint is a welcome comfort when I know change is coming. I just don't know to what end yet. And besides, Caleb is just coming to get his ladder, right? I eye the small cooler dubiously, which suggests more than just a quick errand.

"What about you?" I ask, belatedly. I eye his empty hand, using coffee as an excuse to look at those slender, strong fingers. "Did you get yourself anything?"

"Nah," Caleb shrugs, "I didn't need anything." His

nonchalance is sexy, and I groan internally as I gesture him in and he heads towards the kitchen.

Wait.

Why is he going into the kitchen? I follow him, completely confused. "What the fuck?" I ask, momentarily forgetting the barrage of feelings whirling inside of me. I really shouldn't be surprised, but I am.

"Remember the sfogliatella I told you about?" Caleb asks, as he places the cooler on my island. He settles in further by beginning to unbutton his jacket. Each button undone reveals his white under shirt. I take a sip of coffee to hide my full reaction of his undressing in front of me. I bite my lip, and Caleb grins at me.

"Yeah." I reply, eager to move on. "Did you finish it?"

"Open the cooler," he replies. His jacket is completely open, leaving nothing to the imagination. I reluctantly shift my gaze to the cooler. Caleb works out right? Because there's no way those abs are the product of baking all day. I scoff internally as I gently place my coffee down and follow Caleb's directions. A to-go box is revealed inside. As I lift it out of the cooler, Caleb moves my coffee to the side so I can place the box gently on the island.

The sight in front of me is a fucking marvel. It is living *art*, and I'm *dying* to take a picture and share it with the world. His miniature sfogliatella is plated with a sugar pulled cup marbled with gold foil and red stained sugar. The perfect sized scoop of mint gelato is portioned into the bowl. A compote is drizzled over the sfogliatella to complete the presentation. Raspberries and pulled sugar disks fill in the white space of the container, and I'm transfixed.

"Caleb," I breathe in. "This is gorgeous."

"Thank you." he replies, grinning.

"Is this all for me?" I ask, inhaling the art before me.

"Yes," Caleb replies, giving me a secret smile. "It's all for you, Rayanne."

"I can have all of it?" I whisper, speechless. I am not prepared for what the dessert offers: time, thoughtfulness, and care. Like everything Caleb does, the intent behind it is to steal your breath away, and I can't even compute. It hurts, the affection he offers me by preparing such a beautiful dessert. I take a moment to breathe in deeply. *In and out.*

If you want it, take it.

Okay, Isla.

I want this.

I want to accept this gift Caleb offers me. I want the thoughtfulness, the time, and care Caleb offers for the taking. I hesitate though, because to what extent am I willing to accept all he offers? To what extent do I share that I want Caleb and all he can provide?

"Yes, sweetheart." Caleb replies, the nickname tugging at my heart. It pulls me away from this gorgeous dessert in front of me. "Can I offer you a bite?"

"Should I start with the gelato?" I reply, eyes falling back down to the plate. I study the dessert longer than it warrants. "It's not going to last long, right?"

"Here." he replies, scooping up a sfogliatella and placing a taste of the gelato for me on top. "You have to combine the flavors together."

"Caleb," I hesitate, awkwardly taking the proffered dessert in front of me. I pause, thinking about why it was made in the first place. It's exclusive and for a menu proposed for New Year's Eve. "Is this even allowed? I thought you were presenting this for the final menu tomorrow."

"Consider it research." he replies, trouble dancing in his eyes. "Any feedback you give me I can apply to the future."

A laugh escapes my lips as I roll my eyes at him and that

trouble that's promised. Leave it to him to take this opportunity to feed me.

"You're such a dork," I laugh at him. I take a bite and all my laughter fades, getting lost in all the combinations of textures and flavors in my mouth. I close my eyes to savor the depth and detail that encompasses the sfogliatella and all it has to offer. The crisp flakey layers of the sfogliatella are coupled with an explosion of raspberry and lemon cream filling. The mint gelato finishes the flavors perfectly. It's simply extraordinary.

There's a reason that Caleb is head pastry chef at a top new restaurant in town. His vision and execution of all he creates is utter perfection. I involuntarily moan in pleasure and snap my eyes open in recognition of my gaff. I shouldn't be making sex sounds in front of Caleb. I finish chewing, then swallow and steady my hand on the island.

Caleb drinks me in greedily. The look of possession in his eyes is unexpected, and I reach out for my coffee, clenching my legs against my response. Here before me, is this *beautiful* man, drinking me in like I'm the sunshine and breath of life he needs. The magic swirls between us, and I know this is a *moment*. Do I accept the pull between us? Because honestly, I've never had a man stare at me like I'm the center of his orbit without feeling overwhelmed. I am completely, one hundred percent cherished by Caleb... but still, I wonder if accepting what he has to offer is worth the risk of everything falling apart.

"What'd you think?" he asks, and the tone in his voice goes straight to my groin. It's deep, husky, and filled with sex. The deadly aim hits me in my center, and I feel a thread of composure unravel at my wanting.

"It's amazing." I make myself maintain eye contact with Caleb. I make myself look at the options in front of me.

You can have it. If you want it.

"I've never tasted anything like it." I finish, and there's sensual warmth to my tone that responds to his own husk and desire.

"Would you say there's an imbalance of flavor?" he asks huskily, stepping into my space and caging me in.

"It was perfect." I whisper, affected by the closeness of his body.

"You might need to try the compote drizzle again." he says, swiping a finger through it and offering it to me.

"It's good. It tastes like raspberries." I reply lamely, blinking up at him through my lashes.

"But did you taste the mint?" he whispers devilishly. He leans in, separating our foreheads by millimeters.

"Mint?" I ask, rather stupidly. Of all the things to comment on… but then again, my mind hasn't exactly been focused on whether the flavors are balanced. "I'll try it with this." I reach for another sfogliatella, swipe it through extra compote and pop it in my mouth before he can offer me his finger again.

The second bite is just as good as the first. The crunch of the sfogliatella is refreshing against the creamy filling. For good measure, I lick the extra compote off my fingers, just to make sure I can say I searched for the mint flavor. It's subtle and balances the fruity flavor with a clean finish.

When I open my eyes, Caleb is in my space again, licking the compote off his finger. The hint of mischief in his eyes, his smile tugging at the corner of his lips melt my panties. *Just* a little.

"Did you find the mint?" he whispers, closing the gap between us, touching his forehead to mine.

"Yeah," I murmur on a breath. "At the end."

"I think you missed some," he replies, touching the corner of my mouth lightly. And before I can respond, he licks it off.

I attempt to turn him away by tilting my face the other direction, his mouth catches mine.

I can't say I'm surprised that Caleb tastes like the raspberries he's just savored. I open my mouth to accept the kiss he offers and find the mint he insisted upon. He traces his tongue on the edge of my lips, asking for permission to kiss me properly. I nibble his lower lip in acceptance, and he sweeps my hair out of my face as he deepens the kiss, sucking on my lip in return. His kisses with an edge of desperation, like all he's wanted was to be here, embracing me. I kiss him back just as readily: because let's face it, I've needed him since I made him walk out the door on Friday.

I moan softly. The tenderness Caleb offers me with his kisses takes my breath away. His attention is just for me. When Caleb Gardiner kisses a woman, he does it with purpose. He takes what he wants—he always has. But to feel the effects of his full court press is truly all encompassing. I gasp, taking a step away.

"Caleb," I'm breathless. "Just… a moment, yeah? I need one of those." I inhale deeply to counter the passion inside me, so ready and eager to match Caleb step by step.

"What is it, sweetheart?" Caleb looks concerned.

"I don't—" I sputter lamely. Unsure of how to process the question and my feelings, I grab my takeout box and walk back to the fridge. Just as I open the door, I find myself scooping up the rest of the gelato and melt as it dissolves in my mouth. It is the *best* combination of cream, sugar, and mint known to mankind. I moan quietly as I shut the door to the fridge. I haven't figured anything out in the thirty seconds I've taken, but at least the space has allowed me a spare moment. A vista of opportunity is before me, and all I have to do is take the chance and leap… if I want it.

When I turn around, Caleb is in front of me on the edge of

my personal space. He lifts one of his arms above me and presses his weight against the refrigerator door. He leans into my space, embracing the chemistry that rages between us. He examines my curves thoroughly, and I can't stop watching him. His need to drink me in is intoxicating. I focus every iota on Caleb, aware of the movement of his breath and how his mouth parts, so he can lick his lips. I feel an arch in my back pull me towards him. When Caleb lowers his head down to whisper in my ear, his hair falls in his face, and I have to bite back my need to brush it from his eyes.

"Rayanne," he murmurs in my hair, finally taking the step into my space and cupping my cheek.

"Caleb," I start, but my voice wavers. I honestly don't know what to say.

Caleb closes the space between us as he wraps my arms around his neck and hugs me tight. I expect him to try kissing me again, but his caress is gentle. Caleb kisses the top of my head, as if he just wants to offer me comfort. The tips of his fingers graze so lightly against my temple, tears well and prick my eyes, begging to fall.

"Caleb—" I whisper again. "I'm not sure—"

"See, here's the thing, Rayanne." he interrupts me, leaning down to murmur in my ear. His voice is quiet, seductive, and enchanting. "You haven't told me that you want me to go, and I think we need to sort out what's between the two of us."

I'm breathless. Caleb is acting faster than I can process my feelings, but he gently releases me from our embrace and tilts my chin up to look up at him.

"Tell me you don't want this, Rayanne," he says, leaning in and caging me against the fridge, an arm over me, his body pressing close. "Tell me, and I'll go." Caleb swipes my hair out of my face and leans down to kiss me. It's soft and inviting.

"Caleb—" I whisper. "I shouldn't—"

"But you do." he whispers, leaning down to kiss me chastely once more. "And we're here."

rayanne

WORST OF ME | JULIA MICHAELS

This is your chance, Rayanne. You can tell him to go —if you want.

Indecision swirls around me, and I'm dying to process my emotions faster. When I look up at Caleb again, the final fortifications built around my heart crumble. He is all patience and desire, longing and compassion. He is an extension of my heart, and I just have to woman up and take what I want. I just need to extend my hand out at his offer, and he will take it and keep me safe.

Caleb waits for my consent. When I finally give in with a nod, he leans down to kiss me again. His lips press gently against mine, then seek entrance as he traces the line of my lower lip with his tongue. I pull him in closer as I wrap my arms around his neck. Caleb presses his body closer to mine and the ache I feel in my body slowly knits my broken parts back together as we hold on to each other.

Caleb skims his teeth against my lips, eliciting a moan from me. I wrap a leg tight around his hips, feeling the motions of my desire rock involuntarily against him. My body knows how to express the thoughts I am unable to say aloud. Caleb responds by gripping my other thigh and raising it with a sweeping motion so that my legs hook around his hips and I'm pressed hard against the fridge. I feel his desire for me as his cock rubs against me despite being fully clothed. Caleb's hips tilt into mine as he sucks on the soft spot behind my ear.

"Is this what you want?" Caleb asks, stilling me into silence once more. "Use your words and tell me what you want, Ray."

I try formulating words and gape like a fish at him. Then I gather myself together, so I stop looking like an idiot.

"You didn't answer me, Rayanne." Caleb taunts the lobe of my ear with his tongue, making me gasp. "Tell me."

The motion of our bodies moving together has ceased even as I'm still pressed against the fridge and Caleb keeps me wrapped around him securely. I hiss with displeasure as I realize we won't move forward without my verbal consent.

"*Tell me*, Rayanne." Caleb urges. "Is this the only kissing we're doing tonight?"

Meaning, *are we done?*

No, we're not fucking done. I scoff with disbelief, then laugh with amusement as he waits silently.

"No!" I finally gasp out. "No, we're *not* fucking done. Are you kidding me?"

"Thank fuck." Caleb groans as he kisses me greedily.

"You are a fucking asshole for even asking." I hiss, while batting his shoulder with my hand. "You know that?" Caleb ignores me as I feel the pressure of his lips suck on the nape of my neck.

"Tell me," He murmurs, a hint of amusement in his voice. Caleb kisses that sweet spot heartily, and I sigh with happiness. He repositions his grip under my thighs and on my ass as he walks us over to the couch. "Are we going to sit on the couch?"

"Yes." I concede, narrowing my glare on him. He can't be up to any good with this line of questioning.

"Good, because you're fucking heavy." He grins, mischief dancing in his eyes.

"Asshole." I punch him on the arm. We laugh together as he falls down on the couch. Then I feel the full length of his desire underneath me, and it's considerable. So much so, that I automatically stop giggling and focus my concentration on not automatically moving against him.

"You don't hate it though, do you?" Caleb smirks as he shifts under me, his body hitting all the right points against mine.

"Shut up, Caleb." I smirk. *Cheeky bastard*. He laughs as he wraps his hands around mine to keep my arms wrapped around his neck. Caleb leans his forehead on mine, nurturing the intimacy building between us.

"I'd rather fuck you." he says with a deep and sensual rasp, as he lifts his hips against my sex. The mood changed into something deep and heady. I act reflexively, rocking into him. I look deep into Caleb's eyes, acknowledging the change and the wanting. Caleb releases my arms from around his neck as he moves with me, pressing his hands into my hips calling all my attention and desire as it builds in my center.

"Yeah *sweetheart*," I groan, attempting to keep some sort

of dignity as I reply sarcastically. "That's not happening." With a wide grin, Caleb grinds against my center and a breathless moan escapes me.

"We can still have fun tonight," Caleb replies with such a carefree smile that I'm unable to contain my own laughter.

He leans to nuzzle my neck with his nose, but I catch his chin with my fingertips so I can kiss him properly. He presses his lips hard against mine and I seek an opening into his mouth with my tongue. Our teeth and tongues clash and dance together as we press our bodies against one another. We kiss for an endless amount of time. It could be hours or days, and it feels like years of embracing one another as we cling to each other. Sometimes a laugh bursts from one of us in wonder at the new changes between us and how natural it all feels.

Our deep connection feels cherished as we make up for lost time. Caleb changes the pace when I least expect it; slowing down and teasing me with long lingering embraces with our tongues and teeth when I kiss him hard, then changes the pace and presses his lips against mine with such desperation that I attempt to fill his ache with my own.

The friction of our hips moving against each other are slow and steady. When Caleb wraps his arms around my shoulders to hug me closer to him, my petite frame fits against his chest like I was made for him. Caleb slowly lifts his hips against mine one more time and any sort of composure I've clung to is officially lost. I kiss him hard, and he tugs my hair gently as he kisses me back with equal fervor.

"I need more." I gasp, tugging at his chef's jacket. "Take this off."

Caleb obliges, taking both his outer layer and tank off. He tugs at the hem of my shirt, and I lift my arms up for him to take it off. He studies me for a moment, completely capti-vated. I thank the lingerie gods that I changed into something sexy and feminine instead wearing of my raggedy Victoria's Secret bra. The lace on my white balconette is a delicate French soft, floral design. The wide double straps complete the sexy design, despite having a modest lift. As Caleb freely soaks me in topless, his eyes glint in appreciation as he sees just how much skin there is to kiss.

"This is gorgeous," Caleb brushes a finger along the strap of my bra, and I shiver with anticipation.

"Thank you," I smile shyly at him. I hum my pleasure as Caleb leans down and brushes his lips along my open chest. The movement of his tongue against my exposed skin opens me up to him. "Caleb!"

I moan feeling the intense movement of his mouth on my skin. I sit up taller, offer more of my neck, and his tongue finds a magical rhythm of licking, sucking, and biting as he moves up my neck. I spread my legs further on his lap and we start another steady movement against each other as he bites down on the crook of my neck. I gasp as he sucks on the same spot and then moves further down my chest. I lift my arms up to offer the exposure of my breasts. Caleb teases the seam of my bra line with his tongue. I'm aching for him to move down, but the sensation of pleasure dies as he stops short of my peaked nipples.

I look down searching for the reason. Caleb smiles gently at me, then brushes my hair away from my face. He's waiting patiently for my approval and consent.

Again.

I scoff with frustration. Surely, I do not need to endure this torture to offer consent for every step. Appreciation swirls with my frustration, as Caleb leans back, hands propped behind his head. Damn his stubborn streak! I'm used to men just taking what they want without asking permission. This patience—Caleb's care for my acquiescence is brutal, but I've also never been as turned on as I am now.

"Fucking, yes!" I groan in anticipation.

Caleb's tongue finds my nipple through the lace and sucks *hard*, and an unrecognizable sound escapes me. He sucks and licks through the lace until my nipple is taut. The brush of lips is gentle, but the pull and pressure of his sucking is the perfect combination that builds me up to a single point of demand, leading to an explosion of pleasure. I press my free nipple between two fingers and Caleb swats my hand away.

"Mine." Caleb growls, as he leaves my taut nipple for the other.

I laugh huskily at his reprimand, then immediately groan, carefree and full of wanting. Caleb's filthy mouth murmurs small vocalizations against my skin that completely ruin my panties. The steady pace of our gyrating hips becomes harder and faster. He pulls me against him as he presses his back into the couch and pulls me closer, changing our position again as I lean over him.

The synchronicity between our bodies demands the question of why we've never done this before. Why haven't I given myself permission to see Caleb as more? Because this feeling… what's between us is sensational. It feels so natural and right that the impression takes my breath away.

I freeze at the thought. The intrinsic movement between our bodies is intoxicating and I'm suddenly very aware of what this all means. There's no stepping back from this—no pretending what we've done hasn't happened.

"Rayanne?" Caleb senses my panic and gently turns my face to his. "Sweetheart, where did you go?"

"I—don't, I'm—" I stammer, unsure where to begin.

"Are you okay?" Caleb asks gently. "Do we need to stop?"

"And if we do?" That question catches my attention because I know how much he wants this.

"Then we had fun," Caleb replies, hugging me close to him. "And we'll do it again if that's what you want."

"Caleb," I sigh, knowing that he understands me so well. That's exactly what I needed to hear. "What am I going to do with you?" I touch my forehead to his, and he nuzzles his nose against mine.

"You could kiss me again," he smiles devilishly. "If you like."

I laugh openly at the hope emerging from him. All of my soft curves pressed into his hard lines, making me aware of just how right this is.

If you want it, take it.

I take a moment to breathe in and out and absorb what's before me. Caleb's hair is sexy as hell, mussed up by my touch. His mouth is parted, waiting with anticipation for my response. I brush a fingertip down his nose as light as a butterfly, then skate my hand down his cheek. I search for a trace of any reluctance lingering inside, but all I find is eager-ness to feel Caleb's lips on my skin once more. I take the whole sight of a shirtless Caleb on my couch. It's a beautiful, rare sight. His muscles are long, lean, and sculpted. His strength is apparent as I feel his biceps wrapped around me. A memory flashes before my eyes of Tuesday, when Caleb changed his t-shirt in the back of his truck.

It was an accident that I noticed, really. He hadn't told me he was taking his shirt off in exchange for a fresh one in the back of his truck. When I saw his exposed and sculpted shoulders and biceps, I had to physically make myself tear my eyes away from the sight. If I had known that he looked that good with a shirt off before, I might have resisted that glance in the rearview mirror.

I press a hand against his chest, remembering that moment fondly. I brush my fingertips lightly against his skin, turning the movement into light circles. My hands shift down as I give a slight tug on his nipple, and Caleb groans softly.

"Ray," Caleb warns.

"Yes?" I smirk devilishly at him.

This is fun.

"Kiss me now, or I'm going to take my chances and kiss you senseless into tomorrow," He growls, and his threat is very appealing.

"You drive a hard bargain, Gardiner." I reply, a smile curling on my lips.

"Ray," Caleb demands. "Kiss me now, or I swear to god—"

I laugh, then run my fingers through his hair. I trace the frustrated line of his lips with a fingertip until it turns into a smile and kiss him softly.

"You are beautiful," I whisper. "Did you know that?"

"Not as beautiful as you are," Caleb replies. "You take my breath away every day." His lips brush the side of my jaw and kisses his way down the shell of my ear. A delicate combination of tongue and teeth against my tender skin elicit a moan from me.

"Are we doing this, Rayanne?" Caleb murmurs against my skin. His lips move away from my neck and Caleb looks at me. "Tell me what you want, and I'll give you everything you ask and more."

"Yes," I reply, cradling his face in my hands. "We're doing this."

"Thank god." Caleb brushes his lips against mine, and I open eagerly for him. As our tongues collide, Caleb presses his hips up against me. His cock rubs against my center as I push down onto him, moaning. We find our rhythm slowly, as he begins to explore my body once more. I run my fingers through his hair, pressing him closer to me. Caleb skates his fingers up my torso and his thumbs brush my nipples into hard buds. He pinches one as his lips finds its way to the other and sucks. *Hard.*

"Caleb!" I moan. "More—give me more."

Caleb softens my body with desire as he works between both breasts, reverently praising each until the brink of ecstasy begins to churn in my center. I run my fingers through Caleb's thick hair and tug his mouth to mine, demanding his lips. As our tongues dance, I drink in the feeling of one of Caleb's hands skating from my bottom to the center of my sex, pressing a thumb against it. An electric storm is rising in my body; my center white hot and demanding. The much-anticipated relief I'm expecting never comes, and I'm forced to focus, making eye contact with Caleb.

"Fuck, Caleb," I groan, grinding against his hand. "Yes. Touch me there. Make me cum."

"That's my good girl," Caleb grins against my skin. He bites down gently on the nape of my neck as his tongue swipes soothing strokes against the rough touch. His thumb presses into my center as the strokes of his fingertips are long and languid. I pull him closer, relishing every shared touch as Caleb's tongue expertly drives wild pleasure into an emerging point of focus. Caleb kisses his way down to my nipples as his attention returns to making them taut once more.

As we move against each other, the pressure of his fingers rubbing against my clit, the onslaught of sucking and nibbling on my nipples hardens the center of my core. Caleb moves longer strokes between my legs as we move. He keeps the pace, pushing against my jeans and on my sex. As the electricity rises from my navel, the hair on my arms rises with waves of pleasure building into a white, blinding light. My moans turn into a scream of pleasure as my body bursts like a supernova. Caleb rides out my orgasm in supplying pleasure until I've seen it through.

"Oh, my god." I gasp.

I look down on Caleb; his grin is as enigmatic as the Cheshire Cat who looks like he's won the cream. *Smug bastard.*

Caleb playfully nips my neck. "*Mine.*"

It takes a moment, coming down from the high, but the word hits me like a freight train. It sets me on edge, and I sit up rather abruptly. "Excuse me!?"

The endorphin high has evaporated and I'm instantly on alert. That possessive word takes me to a dark place I try to forget. I've worked hard to pick myself up from that difficult headspace. I don't need, nor do I want, any reminders of where I've been in the past.

"Mine."

Even as Caleb looks at me so fondly, and even as my heart beats loudly for him in my chest, a cold wave of emotion rolls over me. I don't like the sound of being someone's—not even Caleb's. All my insecurities and reservations immediately come to the surface.

Tonight was a mistake. That kiss on Friday was a mistake. I should never have listened to Isla. I shouldn't have given in to my selfish desire for Caleb, because now he actually thinks he has a chance with me. My mind clears away the haze of indecision and doubt. Any lingering questions I have in my mind about Caleb, and what to do with these feelings stirring within me vanish.

Stupid, Rayanne—this was very dumb of you.

"No, Caleb." I remove myself from his lap and step away from him. "I don't think so. You don't get to claim me like that."

No one does.

I let someone claim me once. I let someone possess my heart and my mind and my body, only to be left behind, shattered in the dust. I am the only person that has the right to

142

those precious pieces. I've worked hard to make sure no one will ever possess me like that again.

"Why?" Caleb asks, rather stupidly. The playful tone has diminished between us, and he looks utterly lost. I get it. I just turned a complete one-eighty on him, but it's my responsibility to let him know that this—whatever's between us isn't going any further than tonight.

"This was fun," I reply, ignoring the question. I find my shirt and tug it back on. I look around for his and toss it his way. "You need to go, Caleb. Thanks for the orgasm."

Be a bitch, Rayanne. Rip the band-aid off so fast so he doesn't have a chance to recover.

"The fuck, Ray?" Caleb replies, utterly astonished. "That wasn't just fucking around. Not for me."

No, it wasn't.

That's the problem, isn't it? I comb through my apartment for all the shit Caleb brought in and gather it at the door. The faster he gets out, the easier my breathing will become. The faster he leaves, the sooner I can begin the process of recovery from whatever tonight has become.

"Rayanne," Caleb corners me in the hallway. "Talk to me, what the hell's going on?"

"I *am not* yours," I spit out angrily. "I will never be *yours* —this, this fucking thing—" I wave my hands around, gesturing between us. "It's not happening."

"Why?" asks Caleb, rather patiently. He crosses his arms across his chest. "You said that, but I don't get it. Talk to me."

I laugh bitterly, feeling the endless swells of emotion surge through me. Does Caleb think that after a week of spending time together makes us a team? Or does he think that because he gave me an orgasm, we're suddenly official? We *are not* official. This orgasm was just a moment of indulgence—a stupid, selfish, overindulgence on my part. I shouldn't have given into my feelings for him. And now I'm stuck here, frozen in the raw intensity of emotions that if I process all I feel right now, I might break down. I'm not breaking down for another man ever again. I'm only now more resolute in stamping out these feelings that have swelled inside of me this last week.

Isla was wrong. I don't get to take what I want because there are too many risks involved with Caleb Gardiner and my heart. I was wrong to take advantage of him and use him for my own needs. I was wrong to think that I could look away from all the barriers that lay between us.

"Ray?" Caleb tries again. "Is it Isla? You know she doesn't care if—"

"I *know* she doesn't care," I reply, spitting out the words like an angry cat. "She actually would like to see us together—"

"She said that?" Caleb asks, a playful grin tugging at his lips. That beautiful smile pulls at my heart strings, and I attempt to shut down the flutters swooping through my body, knowing that smile is just for me. "When?"

"It doesn't matter," I reply, waving it off. "We aren't a thing that's happening."

"Why? Because Isla's my sister?" Caleb asks. "If she's told you she's okay with us, it shouldn't matter, right?"

"You know you can be rather short-sighted, Caleb?" I snap, sick of the feelings twisting inside of me. We clearly don't see eye to eye. The fact that he's always felt so strongly about me blinds him to the reality in front of us. It blinds him from the trouble that comes from falling for a family friend.

"I can be short-sighted?" Caleb parrots my words with raised eyebrows.

"Yeah," I reply, crossing my arms over my chest.

"*I* can be short-sighted?" Caleb laughs. "Jesus Rayanne, that's rich coming from you."

"This will never work!" I shout angrily, pointing between

us. "Sorry to burst your bubble, Caleb, but we aren't falling in love and living out a happily ever after." The words burst from my mouth against my will, and I know I can never take them back.

"Why?" Caleb demands. "Because you're wondering who will pick up the pieces if we fall in love and break apart?"

Exactly.

"Because if we do fall in love and I break your heart, Isla will have to pick between us?" Caleb scoffs angrily, running his fingers through his hair. "Jesus, Ray—"

His words hit the *fucking* bull's eye.

"I'm not making Isla choose between us, Caleb." I reply, resting my hands on my hips. "I love her too much."

"Give me some credit, Rayanne," Caleb rolls his eyes. "Don't think for one second that I don't know the treasure you're worth. You don't think I've run through all the possible outcomes in my head? Don't you know I understand the risks involved with your heart? I *know* what you've endured."

I step back, feeling the impact of his words. Even in his frustration, Caleb's first thoughts are for me. This isn't good —it can't be. God, he needs to find a way to turn off those feelings and instincts to care for me. And if, somehow, Caleb is attempting to connect what's between us and my ex, that's ridiculous. This is why our boundaries should never have been crossed.

"This isn't about Isla," Caleb replies, running a broad hand over his face. "She's not the real problem here, Rayanne."

"No?" I raise my brows with disbelief.

"No." We stare at each other at an impasse. Caleb looks at me expectantly, waiting for me to take the bait, but I'm not following through. I scan the apartment for his chef's jacket and pick it up.

"It's time for you to go," I tell him, shoving his jacket in his arms.

Caleb hasn't moved to put it on. He's only looking at me pleadingly, begging me to ask the question. I'm not a fucking idiot and I refuse to engage further in the conversation. I turn away from him to open my apartment door for his departure. The tension is slightly interrupted as he moves to take his chef's jacket.

Finally.

"You know I would never leave you, right?" Caleb interrupts the silence between us, as he sweeps his jacket on. He steps into my space, turns me around, then caresses the hair in my face away from my eyes gently. The touch is so delicate that I feel my body tremble. "I *will* never abandon you. Not like he did."

Oh no, he did not.

"You know Caleb," I reply, pointing a finger at him in accusation. "You can fuck off straight to hell."

"You don't think I saw the aftermath?" Caleb finally explodes. He's been so careful, checking himself this whole time. Caleb has been so patient and considerate of me, but now all that careful thoughtfulness has shattered as he demands my full attention. "You don't think I watched your family and Isla put you back together, piece by piece? Do you not understand how devastated I was for you?" Caleb cuts himself off, breathless with anger. A tinge of sadness shadows his eyes, his brows furrowed with sadness.

He's kept this in for a long time and I've had no idea that these feelings have festered for so long. I didn't know he saw everything fall apart.

"Fuck, Ray—" He sighs and sweeps a thumb across my cheek. "I was broken too. And I had no place to say anything at the time—but I can now."

"A week of spending time alone together doesn't mean

you can comment on my life or what I've experienced." I reply, bracing myself against the warmth his words spread through me. I step back, curling my arms instinctively across my middle. "I don't need to listen to you sharing your feelings or telling me you've pitied me for the past three years." I point a finger at him accusingly. "I don't need you to pick me back up after I've fallen. I'm *fine*, alright? *I* put myself back together."

"Yes, you did, Rayanne." Caleb concedes, but he's still demanding that I see his compassion—or whatever. "Do you not see that I get it?"

I hear him, but these aren't the words I want to hear. He doesn't need to coddle me with his sympathies and understanding. "Caleb, you aren't listening—"

"No, Ray!" Caleb shoots back. "You're the one not listening. We—"

"There isn't a '*we*', Caleb!" I shout, throwing my hands explosively in the air.

"So that's it, huh?" Caleb snaps back. "Well, I'm not here to tell you that I feel sorry for you—I'm not showing you pity. *Fuck pity*, Rayanne. I fucking *hate* that word. I'm telling you that I broke alongside you when you couldn't put yourself back together."

I scoff with indignation, "Right—"

"My fucking crush would never let you take me seriously and I wasn't allowed to say anything, even if I wanted to." Caleb interrupts. "Did you not see at any point, or know how much I was dying to help?

"But this, whatever's between us is more than just a one-sided crush." Caleb shares a pleading look at me to acknowledge what he thinks is the truth. "You and I are real. This magic and chemistry and everything we share—they're *real*. And we're good for each other. How many times have we picked each other time and time again?"

Oh god—too many times. The well of emotion bursting through me is at breaking point, and I resolve to turn the softness I feel for Caleb into a fortification made of diamonds. There is just simply, too much at stake.

"I'm not talking about this," I reply, curling my arms instinctively across my middle. "There isn't an *us*." I hiss.

"Fuck Ray!" Caleb yells finally. "Of course, there is!"

"No, there really isn't." My mind is starting to shut down as my heart stutters. Caleb has to stop talking.

But of course, he doesn't.

"I'm not going to sit here and pretend that I can't connect the dots, Rayanne." Caleb replies so gently, the words caress my skin. His softness is a balm to the rigid ball forming in my stomach. I pause my fury enough to listen to him—just for a moment. "I get it, okay? I really do. Damon was a sickness that infested your soul and tried to take away any beautiful light that makes you shine."

"Caleb," I whisper, unwanted emotions of dread stirring within me. "You. Need. To. Leave. Now." I've resolved to not think of that name, but there: he's gone and done it. He's brought up the shadows I've tried to forget. I will never forgive him for uttering *that* name.

Never.

"No sweetheart," he carefully envelops me in his arms. "I'm not going anywhere. I'm right where I belong." I bristle at his touch and am stiff in his arms, reluctant to accept the comfort he offers. But Caleb gentles his touch, and it's so soft that I feel myself settle into him slowly. I count my exhales, waiting for my heart to stop banging in my ribcage and Caleb holds onto me so long that my arms finally wrap around his waist. A soft kiss brushes against my hair and the fortifications crack open. Caleb hugs me so long that the pieces falling apart inside of me get pulled back together. Tears escape, and I hastily try to wipe them away. The warmth emanating from him reminds me to breathe. Caleb runs his fingers through my hair, kisses my forehead chastely, and squeezes me tightly.

"Are you okay?" Caleb finally asks, brushing a finger down my cheekbone.

"Not really," I laugh, shakily.

"God, Ray." Caleb pronounces as he looks at me. "You're such a fucking treasure." He pulls me back into a hug with such ferocity that my breath is knocked away. He lowers himself to his knees and wraps his arms around my waist then looks at me with those damn puppy dog eyes. "You know that, right?"

Am I?

The question in my eyes gives me away as Caleb laughs bitterly. "Fuck Ray, do you not see yourself clearly?" His hand moves up my torso in a gentle caress, sending shivers down my spine. "You are all strength, and courage, and kindness. You have endured hell and walked out of it standing tall. I'm so fucking proud of you. I'm on your side. You know that, right?"

Despite the loss of breath I feel and despite the fact that this all feels like a dream, his words break down any residual fortifications again. How is it that Caleb Gardiner knows all the right words to soothe my soul and warm my heart? I shudder a breath, looking up to the heavens. I can't…I can't do this. I don't know if anything he's said about my ex is right. But I can't tell facts from feelings or what's right or wrong right now.

Caleb stands up and hugs me briefly. "I'm sorry that this has turned you upside down, but I'm here, Rayanne."

"I know you are." I sigh. He always has been, and that's the hell of it, isn't it?

"Can you do something for me?" Caleb smiles and my heartstrings tug once more.

"What's that?"

"Shine bright, Rayanne Lee Miller." He takes a deep breath, pursing his lips as if he wants to say something more, but holds it back. Caleb swipes a thumb against my cheek, and I involuntarily lean into the touch. I feel a gentle kiss on my forehead then the loss of his warmth. I wrap my arms around my middle to try and hold myself together.

Caleb picks up the ladder and small cooler as he opens the door to leave. After all the demands I've made that he leaves my apartment, he's finally exiting the door and I *fucking hate* it. I don't want him to walk away. I should never want to see him again as Caleb has crossed a line that's hard for me to forgive. But his gentleness and love make it feel like he hasn't betrayed me.

My heart pounds hard against my chest and against my wishes. My soul demands his return. I want his arms wrapped around me and I want his warmth to comfort me and cradle any insecurities I feel. I want his arms to be the blanket that wraps around me and never lets me go.

But he steps out of the apartment, and I follow after him. I watch Caleb walk down the stairs of my apartment complex. The ensconces guiding him down the stairwell reflect the light on his face in the shadows. He looks back at me with such fondness that I can't help but believe him. I want to trust that he'd never hurt me or leave me. If I felt like I could give my heart away, it would already be his. But I've already learned that hard lesson, and the risk of losing Caleb is enough to harden my heart. *I must.* For better or for worse, Caleb is in my life because he's Isla's kid brother, and I will not risk what good is already between us.

I step back through my apartment and close my door. I lean against it heavily, letting it hold my weight as I fall to the floor. A heavy sigh escapes my lips and sadness overwhelms me. Caleb is wrong. He has to be. What's between us has passed and we'll never work out.

As much as my heart aches for Caleb Gardiner, I'll never allow my desire for him to show again.

epilogue: caleb

I THOUGHT SHE KNEW | *NSYNC

I glance back at the Christmas tree in Rayanne's living room before I leave her apartment. Despite how large it is or how much it fills up her living room space, it is breathtaking. It could only be so, as it's the vision Rayanne created by her own sheer determination. On Friday, I checked the tree base again to ensure that the tree would not fall again. Had it not been for this tree, I'm not sure I would have ever had the hope to see my dreams come true today.

Had it not been for this tree, Rayanne and I wouldn't have ever kissed, or made out like our lives depended on each other's pleasure.

153

Had it not been for this tree, I wouldn't have seen Rayanne search through her emotions, opening doors and discovering how deeply she feels for me. We wouldn't have fought about the future—or her past. The mask she wears is so discreet, I'm not even sure she knows she's wearing one. But I see right through it. I know there are parts of Rayanne that suffer every day from the repercussions of her relationship with her ex. I knew better—knew it was too risky to bring up the elephant in the room that was clearly staring at me. But I did it anyway because she needs to know that I see *all* of her and that I want her just the same.

Her ex had too much charisma and sensuality. He also had the dangerous ability to wrap Rayanne around his fingers so tightly that she lost herself in him. She became his perfect barbie doll in beauty, mind, and spirit. Then he fucking abandoned her without a word. No texts, letters, or emails. No phone calls. It was like he had never been there in the first place. After three years of being wrapped up in his world so exclusively, Rayanne was shattered into tiny pieces when he disappeared. She became so lost that she didn't know who she was before she met him.

I hate him. I hate what he did to Rayanne, if only because she's still recovering. It was devastating watching her fall apart. She was only shadows for a long time with his disappearance. It's only been within the last year that she became the sparkling ray of light I've always known her to be.

Rayanne's fear of us and of what we could be is justified. I saw the shadows of her ex hover over her of which I'm sure she doesn't think are surrounding her. When I demanded that she address the reality in front of her, Rayanne shut down. I wish she hadn't. But all I saw from that outcome was that Rayanne has more healing to go through. And I'll be there at her side as she continues to heal—whether she wants it or not.

We are the perfect complement to each other, and if there's anything I've learned this week, it's that my deep intuitive understanding of Rayanne is right. There isn't much I'm good for in this world, but if there's one thing I know how to do right, it's how to love Rayanne Lee Miller.

My phone buzzes in my pocket. It's been several hours since I've left Rayanne. I'm restless in bed, unable to settle into sleep. I wish I could give her the words of comfort I know she needs, but I've known her for so long that I know only Rayanne can sort through her stubbornness and accept the truth. I tap my phone to see that it's her texting me.

RAY MILLER

The sfogliatella is a fucking marvel, Caleb.
You make living art, and I'm so proud you.

CALEB GARDINER

Thanks Ray.

RAY MILLER

You're welcome.

I take a moment to consider if I should address what happened tonight. I'm so tempted, but I don't want to push her away. I know she felt the magic between us. It's always existed, but now she's aware. I think she knows I'll do whatever it takes to earn her acceptance. I'm about to start typing as much when another message flashes before me.

RAY MILLER

You should forget me, Caleb.

Forget us. WE are not an option.

CALEB GARDINER

Never, sweetheart. I'll never walk away from you. Don't you know that by now?

155

I can hear Rayanne sigh across Austin. The thought makes me smile sadly. The response from her is faster than I anticipate. It's all I need to know that she's just as absorbed in our conversation as I am.

RAY MILLER

I know.

Still...

I pause, waiting to hear more, but that's all that comes from her. I know she's gripping her phone tightly, holding onto whatever it is that's piecing her together. I wish I could comfort her right now. As the silence deepens, I carefully compose my feelings into thoughts and pray that she understands why I'm not walking way.

CALEB GARDINER

I know that you think this is a mistake, Rayanne. But it's not.

Whatever your fears are, I will protect you from them.

Whatever your desires are, I will help you fulfill them.

The three dots start moving, but before she can finish her response, I complete mine.

CALEB GARDINER

We aren't done, Ray.

This is just the beginning.

I'm not going to give up until she is one hundred percent mine. If you'd asked me a week ago whether I thought I'd ever make out with Rayanne Miller on her couch, I would never have believed you. And if you had asked me if it was because of a Christmas tree that was too fucking big, I would have laughed in your face. But thank god for that Christmas tree, because otherwise none of this would have happened.

I am the bottom line that cannot be washed away, regardless of Rayanne's protests and fears. It doesn't matter if it takes a month, a year, or the rest of my life. I have the patience needed to earn Rayanne Miller, her trust, devotion, and love.

I will earn it.

the trouble with presents

A SECOND EPILOGUE

Merry Christmas Caleb

rayanne's present

Pictures of You | The Cure
My Hero | Foo Fighters
Robbers | The 1975
Dismantle. Repair. | Anberlin
How Soon Is Now? | The Smiths
Blame Me! Blame Me! | Anberlin
Delicate | Taylor Swift
Pessimist | Julia Michaels
crushcrushcrush | Paramore
Lovesong | The Cure
Misery Business | Paramore
Dance. Dance | Fall Out Boy
3 Libras | A Perfect Circle
The Anthem | Good Charlotte
Hands Down | Dashboard Confessional
There Is A Light That Never Goes Out | The Smiths
Empty Space | James Arthur
The Kill | Thirty Seconds To Mars
Sucker | The Jonas Brothers
Sorry | Beyonce
London Calling | The Clash
Supersonic | Bad Religion
Stolen | Dashboard Confessional
Savior | Rise Against
The Alchemy | Taylor Swift

listen on spotify

rayanne

CHRISTMAS EVE

 hadn't planned to do Christmas with Caleb this year. Not after... well, everything. Yet, here I am, waiting for Caleb to knock on my door because the Christmas spirit is a tricky bastard.

Not literally. But it's been so much harder to forget him—forget what's between us—I find myself expecting to hear his assertive knock on my front door followed by his entrance, making his commanding self at home in my personal space.

The false sensations of Caleb entering my apartment have led me to expect him at any time which must have dug its claws into my psyche, because the musical harmonies we sang together from *3 Libras* has begun living rent free in my mind. His devilish smile and the countless ways he tugged on my hair while we laughed and sang as we decorated my Christmas tree demand acknowledgment. I've been wrestling with these memories since I watched Caleb walk out the door. They've been locked down as core memories, and I've been fidgeting and unsettled ever since.

In my dreams, when the music came, so did Caleb.

It's not like the one where I found peace with my body wrapped around his. No, these dreams were based on the friendship that came with knowing each other for most of our lives. These dreams carried the weight of support, laughter, and friendship. I woke up with the loss of Caleb's acceptance this morning and instantly curled into a ball, trying to hold myself together.

I shouldn't feel so hurt that I changed my mind. I stand by my final decision and will hold my ground that we will never work. And besides, I don't need him for my happiness... *even if* he's felt like another extension of myself at times. *Even if* I hug myself and pretend it's his arms around me. I won't change my mind on shifting my relationship with Caleb into something... more.

But the music sang in my ears, and the dreams clung to my subconscious for so long that I found myself digging through my Spotify lists all day today. I combed through all the songs I have in common with Isla, went through each concert that we attended together, then hoarded all the songs that reminded me of Caleb like a chipmunk hoards nuts in the fall.

The playlist runs for hours. It's just music that soothes my soul, like the way cookie dough satisfies one on a bad day. Before I knew it, I found myself making a separate playlist for Caleb. I grabbed my CD converter for my laptop and pulled up iTunes to burn a physical copy for him. It's dumb, I know. No one actually listens to CDs anymore and I don't even know if he has a CD player to enjoy it. But it's the gesture that counts, right?

I spent hours making the perfect playlist: listening to the transitions of each song's beginning so that it could merge into the next one with perfection. I shuffled the songs for hours until I found the perfect opening and ending. I had an hour and ten minutes for the playlist, and even I have to admit, it's amongst my finest. When I was done, I made sure the Spotify list included some honorable mentions I couldn't fit onto the CD.

I can't explain the intention of the CD that's in my hands… but the aching pain inside dulled a little. Taking action and doing something has brought me inner peace, and perhaps offering him a gift would ease the hurt inside. The weight of possibilities sits heavy in my hands as I look at what I've created for Caleb. The musical memories live on repeat in my head. I don't know what this means symbolically by offering Caleb the CD. I mean, it doesn't have to mean anything right?

I scoff internally, calling bullshit on myself. Making the CD was soothing. The flurry of hurt settled, easing my breaths because I just gave myself an excuse to see Caleb again. The simple fact is that I just desperately miss Caleb, no matter how resolved I am to keep our relationship as it is.

If I could find a stupid excuse—like a Christmas present so I could see him again—I'll do it. I just need to message him now.

I pull out my phone and tap on Caleb's name. Then I take a deep breath and start slowly tapping out the message one letter at a time. My breathing becomes deeper and smoother. When I close my eyes, the harmonies soften into the sweet memories and I'm completely at ease, knowing he'll be here tomorrow.

caleb

CHRISTMAS EVE

Rayanne Miller has made it clear that she doesn't want anything more from me. She's attempting to nip the budding rose of our relationship before it can grow because she's afraid of change. I understand that, and I know why she's afraid. But it's not in my nature to stand aside and let opportunities pass me by if something catches my eye. It's Christmas Eve and I'm getting that last minute shopping done for Isla and mom's "save for last" gifts, a tradition we've kept since we were kids. We'll have a small family celebration when Isla and Graham return from London just after New Year's Eve.

I'll admit I shouldn't even be looking for anything for Rayanne, but she has always been at the forefront of my mind. And even as I'm shopping for a new charm for Isla at James Avery, a necklace of four stars shouts out Rayanne's name to me. I can't help but investigate further as I lower my head to look closer at the necklace. It's beautiful, simple, well-crafted sterling silver with the stars descending in size. It reminds me of shooting stars in the sky. The stars nudge me on, speaking to me like they know who they're meant for.

It keeps whispering, *This is who you are*.

A message solely for Rayanne and where she is in her life. I don't care if the necklace was over a hundred dollars, *this* is an opportunity. It's a moment to share with Rayanne; a reminder that she needs to know who she is, and that I see her *exactly* as she is.

And I love her all the same.

Because I do love her. There is no recovery or going back from spending a week of sharing your heart on your sleeves. You don't *just* recover from offering yourself as a wide, open book to the one person that knows the depths of your heart and soul. You don't walk away from the person who always owned your heart only to dismiss the found chemistry as mere circumstance.

Nah man, I worked hard for that moment—the one where Rayanne saw how well we complimented each other—that we were happy, if only for a few hours together. When she allowed herself that moment of indulgence, she was truly content. And she took exactly what she wanted. Forgive me if I say fuck off to the *maybe's* and the *later's,* as I'm seeing this thing between us through to the end.

A sales associate notices how closely I'm examining the star necklace and shows me a set of earrings and a matching ring to complete the set. A part of me is tempted to buy it all, but it's the seventeen-inch necklace that speaks to me the most. A cluster of stars on her neck will do well to serve as a gentle reminder of how she's seen by the world by those who know her best, including myself. More importantly though, it's a request for Rayanne to acknowledge that even in the darkest days, that light can be found if you keep walking through it.

Rayanne *is* the light that shines in the darkest moments. Whatever she's feeling now won't last forever. She *will* break through to the other side. I tuck the necklace in the pocket of my jacket when it's purchased and pause before opening my text message exchange with Rayanne. She never responded to my last text, my promise that what's between us is just the beginning. A part of me is disappointed, but I know that she needs the time and space to process her feelings.

I turn left to exit James Avery and lean against the wall, only to continue staring at the text exchange. Was it only two days ago that I told her we weren't done? It feels like months have stretched in the last forty-eight hours. Rayanne's necklace sits heavy in my pocket. There isn't regret for the purchase, but I don't know when I'll be able to give it to her. I don't expect to see her at least until Isla and Graham return. It would be the most logical time to give it to her. Perhaps enough time would pass by then that she wouldn't fight me on accepting the gift purchased for her.

I'm still staring at my phone like an idiot, contemplating on whether or not I should text her. As if beckoning her, my phone vibrates with a message from Rayanne. I blink away my surprise when I tap on my phone and an invitation to go back to Rayanne's for Christmas stares at me.

RAY MILLER

Hey… so, I made something for you. Can you stop by Christmas Day?

CALEB GARDINER

Rayanne Miller, are you threatening me with a good time and a Christmas present?

I grin helplessly as I reply immediately. I can see her rolling her eyes at me, that small smirk of a grin turning up on her lips as she suppresses her amusement. The relief I feel from hearing from her is immediate, and I relax my shoulders. I didn't know they felt so tight.

RAY MILLER

No dumbass, just the present.

Are you free?

CALEB GARDINER

I'm doing Christmas with the fam when Isla and Graham return from London.

So yeah, I guess so.

I feel breathless as my heart pounds watching the three dots move. Does this mean I won't have to wait until after New Year's for Isla and Graham to give Rayanne her gift? I've never felt like such a clinger in my life. I let a loose breath of relief when she's confirmed that I'm seeing her tomorrow.

RAY MILLER

Then I guess I'll see you Christmas night.

7pm work for you?

CALEB GARDINER

Hope you're hungry.

I'm bringing snacks.

rayanne

Why won't this damn restless energy leave me? I spent the whole day fixating on making the perfect CD for Caleb, only to confirm that he'll bring snacks tomorrow.

Of course he will.

I shouldn't be so surprised, but I am. I'm glad I started working on that CD for him for Christmas… but it's making me question if it's enough.

I pace my kitchen floor with heavy expectation, knowing that the snacks Caleb will bring me are something sweet. They'll be a labor of love—because that's what he does. Caleb Gardiner doesn't do anything half-assed, and we both know I have the worst insatiable sweet tooth. But if he brings me sfogliatella, I swear to god, I'm shoving him out the door and we can exchange gifts next year.

That memory is still too raw and brings up feelings that feel torturous to remember… like the way I fit perfectly into his body and the way we kissed, as if we had all our lives to explore one another when we pressed our bodies together—

No!

I can't—

It just fucking hurts *too* much.

I begin my pacing along the length of the kitchen, eyeing the counter space that lines my kitchen wall. It's neat and clean, and I have enough space to roll out cookie dough to make my favorite Christmas cookie shapes.

Well, there's an idea.

I grin as I open my pantry doors and refrigerator to study my ingredients for the recipe I know by muscle memory. I quickly pull out the butter and eggs needed, then begin hunting for all the ingredients I need: flour, baking powder, salt, vanilla, and sugar. I assess the line of ingredients before me, noting that the corn syrup is missing for the icing. I grab a small bowl for water to set to room temperature.

Do I have enough time to do this? The icing will take at least twenty-four hours to settle, and even though I don't have to, refrigerating the dough for hours makes the best cookies.

I grab my car keys, resolved to make this work. Perhaps this time I can make something for him just as sweet in return.

caleb

I t's quiet in Austin today. Everyone is with their families or partners celebrating the holiday. I stopped by mom's this morning to give her a kiss and share breakfast with her. In a true Christmas spirit, Mom and I shared a gift together. The theme seemed to be kitchen based, as she got me a couple of insane professional chocolate molds for messing around with. I presented to her a new paring knife which has a matching chef's knife she doesn't know about yet. She shouldn't be surprised in the future when I pop over to her place to cook more often because those Wüsthof knives are top of the line. Besides, it's an easy excuse for me to spend time with mom.

Over breakfast, mom asked how Rayanne was doing, and I'm not going to lie. I stumbled over the question. The knowing look she gave me all but confirmed that she's suspicious of our relationship changing. I won't fess up to anything about us until Rayanne and I know ourselves. I tried to hightail it out of there fast, because my mother is a master at discovering secrets. And while I have nothing to kiss and tell about yet, I refuse to divulge the changes that happened this week. When I kiss mom goodbye, I head over to the restaurant.

Is it a surprise that I'm in the kitchens of *Les Portes de Plaisir* on Christmas Day finishing off the final touches to some of the most decadent Christmas cookies known in Austin?

Not at all.

Are they for work?

Yes, they are, but I'm hoarding two baker's dozens of cookies for Rayanne, knowing she'll eat them through the new year.

The best thing about being a professional pastry chef is having a huge kitchen at my disposal with world class industrial ovens, cooling racks, and counter space. I can literally prepare multiple recipes with my co-workers at a time and use the kitchen whenever I need it. And Luc lets me, in the name of restaurant business. I was really tempted to start experimenting with some of the chocolate molds mom gave me, but I didn't have the sort of time needed to do it well. Not when I had cookies to hand off to Rayanne.

I was always a showoff with my Christmas cookie baking prowess—even before I went to culinary arts school. My teachers in school would start asking when to expect Christmas cookies *before* Thanksgiving. It was an ego boost to say the least, and I'm pretty sure my eleventh grade English AP teacher rounded my grade for the semester up to an A-, simply because I spent a week offering different cookie recipes I made all through December.

Did I actually *bribe* my teacher with cookies?

No—not at all… Swear on my non-existent boy scout's heart.

I've spent the last couple of weeks crafting a combination of classic holiday cookies, including Macaroons, Millionaire Shortbread, Linzer Stars, mocha peppermint fudge,

Polvorones (Mexican Wedding Cookies for you plebeians out there), White Chocolate Peppermint Rugelach, and my chocolate chip cookies recipe incorporating nutmeg, orange, and toffee. Things like the fudge and Rugelach have been prepped in advance, so I'm not pressed for time. I spent the last couple of days focusing on recipes that have shorter lifespans like the Polvorones and chocolate chip cookies. My time spent in the kitchen now is ensuring that I have exactly what I need for Rayanne.

When I mastered the Toll House chocolate chip recipe, I adapted it to incorporate more complex flavors. Somehow the combination of orange and toffee with the nutmeg became an obvious Christmas gift, and that's when I started making them regularly. But that particular recipe became a favorite so fast that I began negotiating rations of cookie dough for Isla and Rayanne's sleepovers. That was the first recipe I truly mastered and has remained a favorite.

Rayanne's collection of cookies includes the shortbread, my chocolate chip cookies, Polvorones, and the Linzer stars. Baking Polvorones was the first recipe I created with Isla and Rayanne when we were kids. We were usually covered in powdered sugar, but the memories created then are lasting.

The Linzer Raspberry Stars are a favorite of Rayanne's. I don't think she can contain her happiness with the jelly filled cookies. Something about the way the raspberry flavor becomes concentrated when it bakes as a cookie always has Rayanne weak on her knees.

I spent more time focusing on the packaging for the cookies than I care to admit. At first it was because I had to find a box big enough to give Rayanne. It was a *task*, but I eventually found something in Luc's office. And then it was the ribbon for the bow. The motherfucking to-go station in the restaurant had *nothing* for what I wanted to give Rayanne. I left the restaurant, hoping that there was an answer in my truck, because it's freaking Christmas Day, and no retailer is open. I sigh a deep sigh of relief as I see a white Michael's bag in the passenger side of truck. I must have remembered yesterday, because the perfect gold metallic ribbon I found is still in the bag. I planned a big presentation with this ribbon —grand enough that would make Rayanne's eyes bulge with surprise.

Worth it.

Knowing that the presentation is exactly as I envisioned is a big relief. I don't care if Rayanne hates me because of that damn bow, it's going to be the best reaction to a gift I've ever received, hands down.

She'll forgive me though.

After all, I'm the one bringing cookies.

rayanne

CHRISTMAS DAY

od, I'm a hot mess.

Between prepping the royal icing and the restlessness that refuses to settle inside, I have gotten little sleep. Who knew that preparing icing could be such a royal pain in the ass?

I spent hours researching hacks and what not to do while prepping it. It's been years since I've attempted to decorate sugar cookies like this from scratch. It's also no thanks to Caleb that I've become spoiled the last couple of years because he's done all the hard prep work I'm attempting to emulate when we gather to decorate Christmas cookies with Isla.

Is this why I'm putting all this effort into baking for Caleb? I spent hours last night getting the right texture and vibrant pigment expected for all colors of the rainbow. The number of times I had to scrap icing because it was too runny is enough to make me cry.

I finally crashed into my bed at three-thirty in the morning after I found my head drooping with exhaustion over the icing on the kitchen counter. Then I startled myself awake at five-thirty because my imagination wouldn't shut up about all the ways interacting with Caleb Gardiner could go wrong tonight.

I'm preparing for every possibility from him royally pissing me off with his smart mouth to restraining myself, so I don't kiss it. Kissing him is not an option. It can't be. Especially when I made myself *very* clear that we would not be changing the dynamic between our relationship. It doesn't matter if I've felt the longing for him, nor does it change the fact that he's still too important to risk losing. If things go wrong—if he falters, or I hurt him, it will end in ruin with Isla being forced to pick a side. I *cannot bear* that future becoming a reality.

I inhale a deep breath and exhale slowly. My nerves are at an all-time high, as it's just on seven o'clock and he'll arrive any minute. I dash around my kitchen, checking on the last batch of cookies, which need about two more minutes. I peek in the fridge to pull out my plate of freshly decorated cookies and frown. The frosting looks muddied, and the colors are blurring into each other. What the fuck happened? They were perfect when I put them in there an hour ago.

An assertive knock on the door makes me jump and I'm convinced my heart skips enough beats that I'm dead on the spot. Caleb's here, and my anxiety has skyrocketed. *Again.*

"Coming!" I shout out to the general vicinity of the apartment entrance. I huff a breath out as I pause to look at the mirror in the hallway.

For fuck's sake, I look like a goddamned Christmas cookie. Dried frosting is smudged on my cheekbones and my shirt is covered in flour. I examine my hands, which are splattered with dried frosting. I don't have time to change *anything* about my appearance.

The door cracks open and I see Caleb's head pop into the apartment. "Ray?" he calls out to the open space. He pauses when we lock eyes as he swings the door wider to let himself in. An upheaval of emotion trembles through me as Caleb makes himself at home in my apartment. It's like nothing has changed since we fought on Sunday. There is comfort in the reassurance of his confidence in us, even if I feel insecure and in denial about what lies between us.

I'm frozen in front of the mirror. I don't know how to act or what to say, because Caleb hasn't changed, and I feel like everything inside of me is bursting with all that's developed since last Tuesday.

"Hey Frosty," Caleb smirks, cupping a hand over my cheek as he rubs excess frosting off my cheekbone.

"Really!?" I swat at him, narrowing my eyes.

"I see you did some baking," he grins as he takes in the mess of my kitchen.

"Ya think!?" I scoff at Captain Obvious, who's taking in the chaos of my kitchen, observing all the various degrees of completion. Out of the two dozen cookies I made for him, only half are frosted, and the last half of the second batch are in the oven—

Oh god.

Oh my god.

"What the—" Caleb crinkles his nose with disgust as he quickly diagnoses the smell as burnt cookies. Even though I'm closer to the oven, he takes two big strides to open it as smoke billows out of the oven. We both start coughing immediately as he continues to wrap a towel around his hand and tosses the cookies into the sink. I head towards the disaster to investigate just how burnt the cookies are and find a small center that still looks deeply golden instead of the crisp black edges.

"Fuck Ray!" Caleb bursts through a fit of coughing. "Use a timer next time, will you?"

"I eyed them just this once!" I grumble, grabbing a spatula to attempt scraping them off the cookie sheet. I don't bother to admit that this mess is my fault because I was freaking out about him being in my apartment again. Or was it because I look like a god damned cookie myself and was trying to recover? It could go either way at this point.

"That whole thing is ruined, sweetheart," Caleb stands behind me, wrapping his arms around me to still my hands. "Cookie sheet, cookies, and all. Better to toss the whole lot in the trash." The impulsive urge to lean into him is strong, and I have to focus every iota of concentration on standing tall.

I huff my disagreement but don't protest. I'm sure he's seen his fill of ruined cookie sheets and baked goods plenty of times.

"So, what's the occasion?" Caleb steps back from me and leans back on the counter with an elbow. The casual elegance of his posture shouldn't be allowed. His face is carefully neutral, but I spot a slight upturn to his lips, revealing his amusement and scowl my annoyance. Why did I think this was a good idea again?

"They're for you," I mumble, unable to make eye contact. "I just didn't have enough time to do it properly."

"For me?" Caleb's grin is wide. "You didn't have to do that."

"I'm beginning to think it wasn't worth it," I grumble. "I officially hate Royal Icing." I only had time to cut out Christmas Tree and Star cookies, especially because I couldn't get the icing right in the beginning. Caleb examines the assorted cookies of varying degrees of completion, finally picking one of the Christmas tree cookies that has blurred icing and smiles at it.

"Yeah, I don't know why the icing looks like that now," I blurt out like an idiot. I'm fully aware of everything I did wrong and am waiting for Caleb to point them out and laugh at me. But he doesn't, and instead takes a bite.

"Fuck, Ray." He groans around the cookie. "Those are actually really good."

"Really!?" I squeal with delight. They better be fucking delicious because they've been the bane of my existence for the past twenty-four hours.

"Yeah, great job." He replies, stuffing the rest of the cookie in his mouth with two bites.

"Thanks." I feel my cheeks grow pink with embarrassment. "Sorry I didn't finish them."

"We can do that together." Caleb steps into my space and strokes strands of my hair that reveal icing in it. *Great.* "After we exchange presents. If you want."

I bite down my automatic *no* because more time spent with Caleb can only lead to trouble. But god, I've been missing him and the extra time with him is only for tonight.

"Sure." Decorating cookies together *has* been a tradition that we've done with Isla every year for the last few years… it would just be us though, and I need to make sure I can handle myself around him.

The smile Caleb offers me is so warm. "Thanks for the cookies." He heads back to the front entrance where I notice a huge to-go box on the ground. It's wrapped with a ridiculous gold bow that my mother would praise with delight. *God, if that's what I think it is…*

I sigh happily as Caleb comes back with the box in tow, knowing that whatever's inside will be far superior to the mess of my cookies. "I promised you some snacks," Caleb says.

"Thank you," I reply politely, then feeling shy all of a sudden. "That's uh—quite the bow you got there, Caleb."

"I made it extra big, *just* for you." He quirks a half smile at me. I scoff loudly while I carry the box to the counter to reveal a collection of my favorite cookies. My eyes widen as I take in that insanely delicious trademark cookie he's made since we were teenagers. He's added Mexican Wedding Cookies, Raspberry Linzer Star Cookies, and millionaire shortbread to the mix. God, I'll be eating these for days.

Show off, I scoff internally.

The various scents of each cookie assault my nose and I'm instantly salivating. Fuck me.

And fuck him, because I'm going to gain fifteen pounds eating every single god damned cookie.

I really should just leave the baking to Caleb. I snatch a Linzer Star Cookie and swoon at the raspberry jam as the buttery cookie melts in my mouth.

"Don't stare at those cookies and judge yours critically," Caleb tilts my chin up to make eye contact. "I *love* that you made cookies for me."

"Even if they're a hot mess?" I chuckle, because it's not just my cookies that are a disaster now.

"Is the icing not quite set? Sure," Caleb shrugs half-heartedly. "Did the decorations get smudged when you put them in the fridge? Yeah, but who cares?"

"But *why*!?" I groan. "They were perfect before."

"Yeah sweetheart, you don't put royal iced cookies in the fridge because of the moisture." Caleb offers me a self-assured grin, sarcastic enough to make his point clear.

Did I read that somewhere? I absorbed so much information while I was baking that I must have forgotten it. I could have sworn I knew that.

"You have enough cookies to last you through New Year's." Caleb winks at me.

This is where I thank him and move on. I should sidestep to the living room and we exchange our presents so we can finish decorating the cookies I didn't get completed on time. But the press of Caleb's fingertips as they tilt my head up, his close proximity, and the intimacy of how well he knows my mind keeps me silent.

This is us now. There is no going back to what was before, and it's killing me inside. I will never *not* want Caleb Gardiner now, because I know how good it can be. I step closer into his space and wrap my arms around his waist. Caleb wraps his arms over my shoulders and breathes my scent in. I am settled and the restlessness has eased. I feel like crying because I've missed him so much.

"Hey you," Caleb kisses my temple and I relax further into his comfort. "I have something else for you."

"So do I." A smile involuntarily spreads across my face while snuggling into Caleb's chest.

"What do you mean!? That mess of a kitchen isn't my Christmas present?" Caleb chuckles and I half-heartedly punch his side.

"You said they were good!" I narrow my eyes accusingly, and Caleb grins appreciatively.

"And they are." Caleb slings an arm across my shoulders and pulls me in the direction of my living room. "How's the tree faring? Still up I see?"

"Obviously!" I pinch his side, and he yelps with surprise.

"Ow! That hurt!" Caleb reaches for me, but I sidestep him. "Come here!"

The temptation to run and play a cat and mouse game is strong, but honestly, there's not enough room to run in my apartment. With my Christmas tree looming over the whole of my living room, it's amazing that I even *have* walking space. I won't admit this to Caleb ever—but I know not to buy a nine-footer ever again. I'll just get an *eight*-and-a-half-foot tree next year. I grin up at Caleb, knowing what I'm planning.

"What's that for?" Caleb looks amused.

"Nothing." I hide my smile from him as I reach for his CD. "Here. Merry Christmas, Caleb."

"Thanks." He rips into the paper and laughs as my play

mix is revealed. "A CD?" He moves in closer so we can read the list of songs together. A lock of hair falls into his eyes and like temptation teases me every time, the urge to move it from his sight beckons me.

Tonight. Just for tonight.

I'm accepting the only present I want.

For now.

I tuck the lock of hair in between fingers, brushing it away. Caleb sighs contentedly at my touch and my fingers curl into his locks. It's just a gentle touch, and a moment of satisfaction, but I let go to pull out my phone. It was enough for now.

"Yeah," I finally reply, as I find the Spotify list and copy the link. "Consider it a symbolic gift, as I'm sure nobody has a CD player anymore." I send him the playlist through text messages.

"This is an amazing playlist," Caleb peruses the list I included.

"There's more," I reply as I text him. "The full list wouldn't fit on the CD, so I put it on Spotify for you."

The sound of a phone vibrating confirms that Caleb now has the whole playlist.

"Seriously, this is amazing." Caleb hooks his hand around my waist and pulls me into him. He kisses the side of my head as I grin shyly back at him. "It's like you went into my head and pulled out all my favorite songs."

It was the music in my dreams that made me do it, but I can't tell him that. It would be a serious mistake to tell him I've been dreaming about him. He might never recover from knowing that, and *I'll* never hear the end of it.

"Here." I feel the weight of a small box Caleb places in my lap. Looking down, it's the classic orange box from James Avery.

"Oh," I shake my head with denial, unable to accept

anything from there. That's solid boyfriend gift giving right there, and I couldn't accept it, even if I wanted to. "Caleb—no, I can't accept this." I try to hand it back to him, but he won't allow it.

"I'm not taking this back, Ray." Caleb says firmly. His hands are wrapped around mine firmly. I couldn't move a fingertip, even if I wanted to. I still try.

"Caleb, this is inappropriate." I grind out. I test shifting my hands out of his with no success. "There is no way I can accept this."

"Bullshit, Ray," Caleb hisses. "Just open the damn present. It's not a ring, I swear."

Well, thank fuck for that.

I would *never* have accepted the present if that was the case.

"Fine!" I reluctantly surrender *for now*. If it's inappropriate, I swear to *god* I'm making him return it to James Avery.

I eye the obnoxious orange box suspiciously like it will bite me. I tentatively release the silk ribbon from the box. Closing my eyes, I exhale through my nose as I open the present, and that's as far as I can get.

"Open your damn eyes, Rayanne." Caleb snorts at me with amusement. "You can't accept it if you don't know what it is."

That's *the* point. I don't want to accept it.

I feel Caleb take one of my hands and place it over the center of the box where the jewelry would be obvious for all. At first, I feel a finely crafted chain. Then, as Caleb guides my hand over the center of the necklace, I feel stars of different sizes joined together. I instantly think of shooting stars when I feel them.

I exhale with relief. James Avery has a plethora of hearts and cheesy jewelry, no matter how finely crafted the silver is.

I open my eyes, absorbing the beauty of four stars in front of me.

Can you do something for me?

Shine bright, Rayanne Lee Miller.

Caleb's words echo in my mind from Sunday. If that isn't a call to arms, I don't know what is. I was too broken to absorb his last few words then, but now it floods my memories, and the tears are threatening to fall.

"This is who you are, Rayanne," Caleb repositions himself in front of me, leaning into my space as he brushes my curls falling into my face. "You are the light in the dark, and you will always shine like the brightest of stars." He leans his forehead on mine, forcing me to stay present with him.

It's too much. I can't accept it.

I *shouldn't* accept it.

Caleb is doing what he does best, addressing the elephant in the room. Suddenly, I feel like I can't breathe as a tear falls down my cheek before I can catch it. Caleb rubs a thumb down my cheek, wiping them away. When our eyes lock, I see just how much of an open book he is, full of emotion. The depth of his affection is immediate, his tenderness is laid bare before me and I close my eyes again, unable to handle what Caleb shares of his mind. Of his heart.

It's evident that this is how he sees me.

"You need to know, sweetheart," Caleb brushes his lips against my forehead. "If you feel lost in a maze of darkness, I *know* you will find your way out. You are too bright to be shut out by the dark. I'll be there for you, whatever you're going through."

God damnit! The asshole has officially gone and thoroughly eviscerated my heart. My tears are falling freely now. It can't be helped. How can I say no to him when he does things like this for me? Caleb's face is neutral, but his eyes give him away as he wipes the tears falling down my cheeks. He's there with me, letting me feel all that's inside.

There's no way I'm recovering from this moment: Caleb's call to action, his unwavering devotion, and silent support breaks me apart and put me back together in one swift movement.

I've officially lost it.

caleb

CHRISTMAS DAY

I don't know if Rayanne has considered the layers of truth I'm lying before her when I give her the necklace. I'm talking about Damon. I'm talking about the fact that she's not as steady as she puts out to the world. I'm talking about the confidence that's more vulnerable than she realizes. I'll stand beside her as each crack in her heart is healed regardless of the time it takes. She might not even realize what's at stake here, and it's okay if she doesn't.

"Can I put the necklace around your neck?" I ask gently, wiping the tears falling down her face. If she says yes, I know she's accepted what I'm offering. I thought Rayanne would be fighting me more. I expected her to put up her walls and draw boundaries between us. She looks like she's been lost in the chaos I know she's suffering through now. From the moment I saw her frozen in front of the mirror in her apartment, I knew she was in rough shape.

I know how much I've missed her. I know the longing I've felt just to reach out to her and share my thoughts. I miss talking to her every day. We connected deeply last week and being cut off from her has me reeling. I'm just glad she seems more settled by my side. Even if she's a hot mess and lost, I wouldn't have her any other way. Rayanne is beautiful like this, and I feel the warmth of her trust in me when she's this vulnerable.

She hasn't answered me yet. I don't know what she's thinking right now, but I ease off my nerves and focus on settling on what she needs right now. If Rayanne needs time to process what I've asked, I can give it to her. I move positions so that I'm sitting beside her and search through the playlist she made for me. As I scroll through the list, absorbing the new additions on Spotify, I marvel at what she's created. She's taken time to craft the perfect playlist, and without needing her confirmation, I know Rayanne took hours making it.

Just as I tap on *Everlong* by the Foo Fighters, Rayanne finally speaks up. "How is it that you see this? How do you know I'm the light?"

My heart breaks for her because now I know just how much work is ahead of her. I silently curse Damon again for breaking her so thoroughly. Is she connecting him to this sadness she feels? I hope part of her is.

"I know," I begin, lacing my hand through hers, "Because that's what you've been for me. When dad left—when shit fell apart, you've been there every step of the way. You guided me out of my darkness, even if you weren't by my side." A fresh sob escapes Rayanne, and I wrap my arms around her. "We've been through it all together. I *see* you, Rayanne. I'm here for you."

"God Caleb," Her cry is anguished. She pulls her hand from mine and covers her face with them. Her knees curl up on the couch and she retreats into herself like a small ball. "I can't with you right now. This is too much—"

Fuck. This is hard. I pull her into my side, stroking her

hair gently, and kiss the side of her head. I offer deep steady breaths to help soothe her. I'm tempted to say something more but decide against it ultimately because she needs time. Whatever I say will be lost to what she's feeling.

"Caleb, what is it exactly that you want?" Rayanne turns to face me, slowly uncurling herself and creating space between us. "What are your expectations here? Because I don't think I can ever be what you need, and I won't change my mind about us."

I sigh, feeling the blow that's intended with that statement. Our dynamic has clearly changed but she's holding onto what we've always been in the past. Do I have any expectations between us? Nothing more than maintaining my patience for all of Rayanne. She's worth the wait.

"For now," I begin. "All I ask is that if you embrace your demons inside, you let me in. Let me help you."

"But you think we'll still end up together," Rayanne replies dryly. She arches a brow in question and crosses her arms across her chest.

"*We've* changed, Rayanne." I point out. "There's no going back from Sunday. And honestly, I don't want to go back to the way things were before."

"But you *expect* our relationship to change romantically," Rayanne drags out a breath. "Why else would you put in this work?"

That's a punch in the gut I didn't expect. I mean, she's not wrong, because I do think our relationship will continue to develop. I think we will become romantically involved. But I don't weigh those expectations with stipulations, and she should know that my intentions are honest, even if they are selfish.

"You're right." I lean back on the couch and look at her steadily. "Yes, I think our relationship will change. But I'm on your time, Ray. I'm not pushing you to feel one way or another. The only thing that I'm asking you is that you let me be in your life. Let me in. Let me be here for you when you need me."

The protest on Rayanne's mouth dies as she processes what I've said. It's almost comical to see her debate with me internally. After a moment, she gazes at me with such sadness I feel it tear my heart. "I can't be what you want me to be for you, Caleb. I can't be your girlfriend."

I remind myself that I already knew this. I knew this was coming. I exhale a short breath, conceding. "Okay Rayanne. I hear you."

"Really?"

I don't think Rayanne expected me to respect her feelings like that. It fucking hurts.

"Yeah, really." I reply, taking one of her hands in mine and kiss the back. "Just know that I'm going to be a really *affectionate* friend."

"You have *no* expectations that I'll change my mind now?" Rayanne asks, brows raised in question.

"Nope," I flash her a grin. "Just as long as you accept that we aren't coming back from this Christmas. I'm showing up for you, Rayanne. Every day, in some capacity. I need you in my life, friend or not. We're doing this. I'm making you dinner every week and leaving you cookies when I go home."

"That sounds amazing, actually." Rayanne sputters a laugh at that. Her smile turns into a disapproving frown as she considers more. "You can't make me cookies every week though, I swear to god I will never recover from all the cookies. This figure you like so much, *will never* recover."

"For fuck's sake Ray," I let out an exaggerated sigh. "I really don't fucking care about that figure you're so worried about. You'd be gorgeous regardless of what size you wear."

"I sincerely doubt that," Rayanne continues to glare disbelievingly.

She doesn't get it, does she? She doesn't see that I honestly could give two shits about her figure.

Yes. Rayanne is sexy as sin.

Yes, I appreciate her figure for what it is now. She's all petite curves and sass for days. But that isn't *why* I love Rayanne Miller. What her figure looks like won't break my affection for her. But the memory of Damon hovers over her and I know that's not been her past experience. I sigh, knowing that this is something she'll have to learn with me in time.

"Can I put the necklace on for you?" I gently prod, changing the subject.

"Oh," Rayanne frowns in thought as she looks down at her lap, studying the necklace. She takes it out of the jewelry box and fingers the stars. A small smile unfurls on her lips as she opens up the chain. "Sure. I actually kind of love the stars."

"I knew you would," I reply, taking the necklace from her. She holds her hair together in a high messy bun that exposes her neck. The line of her skin is tempting, but I resist acting other than to place the necklace around her neck. "Let's see then." Rayanne turns to face me with that small smile on her lips. "Stay there for a sec."

I grab my phone and snap a photo of her, just as she is. Curly hair gone wild, frosting still sticking to her face, but the smile on her face is genuine, even if it is small. My god, she is beautiful. I show her the photo and she shrieks at me.

"God, Caleb, I look awful!"

"You really don't," I reply, gaze steady on hers. I feel her fingers nestle into mine, as her eyes soften. "You're always beautiful."

Rayanne bites her lip, clearly unsure of how to react. I want to tell her that she could eat fifteen pounds of cookies every day and I'd still think she's beautiful. But I stay quiet.

"Do you still want to decorate the rest of your cookies?" I ask, nudging her in a different direction. The "with me" is implied in the question, hoping that she still says yes. A small smile quirks up on her lips as she stands.

"Yeah, that'd be great." Rayanne muses. She offers me a hand up, which I obviously take. "I'm sorry Isla can't join us this year. It's usually all of us decorating together."

I'm not sorry that my sister is out of the country meeting her English boyfriend's friends and family. None of this would have happened if Isla had been here. But Rayanne likes traditions to stay the same, so I understand why she's saying this.

"Come on," Rayanne tugs me in the general direction of the table. "We should figure out what icing is still good. Everything's in the fridge. It's been over twenty-four hours now, so it should have settled. I just want to make sure we can use everything." She's prattling on because she's nervous. I don't think it occurred to her that we could exist in a space with my feelings out in the open and still have a semblance of normalcy between us. Relationships exist in the gray spaces all the time, but for Rayanne, who's always had clear lines established, this is hard. Especially between us: she's made clear that we have strict boundaries and fought her attraction to me. I don't know for how long now. But the magic in our chemistry has always been brewing.

Rayanne shuffles through her fridge, trying to sort through all her various icing colors. A rainbow is piling up in her arms as she gathers all the icing. I smirk at her inability to do anything half-assed. She's nothing short of remarkable with all that she's accomplished in twenty-four hours. Sugar cookies with royal icing take time to plan and prepare. With Rayanne's quick thinking I would have expected her to make one or two colors for decorating.

Nope. She's gone and made the whole damn rainbow.

Rayanne's cursing about new icing that's sticking to her arms and her shirt. I step in finally, taking everything in her arms and placing them on her kitchen table. Rayanne looks surprised when I take them from her, like she didn't expect me to help her arrange and organize the cookie decorations. My jaw clenches and I resist grinding my teeth. Even now, after all this time, Rayanne doesn't expect the men in her life to assist her with small tasks. And I know why.

Her fucking ex-boyfriend didn't do a goddamned thing to help her with things like this. I'm going to fucking kill the bastard if I ever see him again.

"Go change," I nudge her towards her bedroom. "Get freshened up and we'll decorate when you get back."

"You don't mind?" Rayanne's eyes widen with surprise.

"No, sweetheart," I try to gentle my tone despite all the fury in my blood. "I'll arrange everything. Take the time you need. The cookies and I will be here when you get back."

"Thanks," Rayanne flashes me a sweet smile before she disappears.

I find her dishware in her kitchen, grabbing a plate for cookies and a few bowls to house the icing and arrange everything on the table within five minutes. I grab a few paper towels, locate toothpicks and sit down to start decorating. I pick out an eight-pointed star sugar cookie and contemplate the design with the royal icing.

Again, I marvel at the variety of icing colors in front of me. Even I wouldn't have attempted the rainbow assortment in twenty-four hours. I start outlining the borders of the cookie with the white icing. Within the cookie itself, I start drawing smaller stars that will become blue, green, pink, and purple. I grab a toothpick to pull the icing in the right direction for the green star but feel a body hurl itself from behind me.

Rayanne's honey almond scent assaults my senses as her

arms wrap around my shoulders, pulling me back into an embrace. I chuckle at her reappearance in the kitchen, but quickly adjust my expression when I turn and see Rayanne's. I've never seen her so vulnerable with determined focus like this. Clearly, she's been thinking, as everything about her has changed from ten minutes ago. I don't know how to interpret where her mind's gone. I adjust my posture to take everything in better, Rayanne climbs into my lap like a little kid needing comfort. I instantly rub her back, kiss the side of her temple and rock her gently side to side.

"What's this, Ray?" I murmur softly in her hair. "Talk to me."

"Yeah. I know." Her voice is muffled by my chest, and I hug her a little tighter. "I'm trying."

"Take what you need," I reply, stroking her hair. "I'm not going anywhere."

The cookie I started decorating has been abandoned on the table as I focus on Rayanne. She's changed shirts, taken off all the extra icing on her arms, face, and neck. She seems put back together, but I'm missing something. And while I love holding her in my lap, I don't know why she's here.

Rayanne finally looks at me, scanning my face and letting me see what's in her eyes. She's searching for answers in my eyes, and I know she's looking for reassurance that's already there. She exhales a shaky breath and tries to relax.

"You mean it?" Rayanne finally asks.

"What specifically are you thinking of sweetheart?" I smile, entertained because it could be anything she's thinking about.

"You'll wait for me on my own time?" Rayanne clarifies, ripping my heart open with hope.

Time has stilled and for the first time I'm speechless. I'm not prepared for this conversation to happen now, assuming she would need more time. "Ray, what's happening here?"

Rayanne exhales steadily. "I've been thinking."

"Clearly," I scoff with surprise. "Tell me more."

"Can you answer that question first?" Rayanne beseeches me. "Come on Caleb, I really need to know if you mean it."

"Always, Ray." I try to instill confidence in my tone, but it comes out as a whisper. Fuck. I am not prepared for this conversation. Do I want to have it? Hell yeah, I do. But I'm not gonna lie, I'm really fucking confused. Where is this coming from? "A little help here? What the fuck?"

Rayanne huffs a laugh and covers her face with her hands. "God, Caleb, I have no fucking clue." I gently lift her face up to mine so I can see her face as she explains. Rayanne visibly gulps, then continues. "I'm still sorting through my feelings and what I want versus what I expect. I just know enough that I think you deserve to know too."

"Just now?"

"Yeah, it was when you let me get changed," Rayanne's cheeks blush slightly.

"I didn't *let* you do anything," I raise a brow in question. "You clearly needed to change."

Rayanne smirks, "Right."

"Okay, so…" I exhale shakily. Rayanne nods, like she's preparing herself for this conversation too. "What's going on in that chaotic head of yours?"

"I'm not making you promises I can't keep," Rayanne begins, stating the obvious.

"Yeah, Ray, I get that." I smirk at her. "I'm not asking you to."

"Stop interrupting, asshole." She pokes my chest and presses a nail into my sternum, which actually hurts. Her eyes blaze with emotion, and I'm not sure I'm prepared for what's about to come. "I'm pissed at you because I actually want this… whatever's between us." At that, I raise my brows and her cheeks redden. "Look, I don't know what comes with that. But I know that these last two days have been utter hell, and I hate it. I fucking miss you and I hate it. I hate how I want you. I'm not thrilled at all the ways this could go wrong. And I'm so fucking pissed at you for making me feel so strongly."

"Ray," I laugh helplessly, unable to help myself because... *what?* "Jesus Christ, I think you might be trying to kill me."

"I'm *sorry*," Rayanne smiles sadly. "Really, I am. You're right though: we can't go back to what we were before. I've been festering in these feelings that have consumed me for days. And I know I'm not in a good place to make you any promises for what you want now. But I can promise I'm willing to try and sort whatever's between us. I just... need time."

"God, Ray." My voice is rough with emotion as I brush her hair out of her face and lift it up to mine. I didn't know hope could feel this good. I would never have asked this of her, but she's offering me everything I've ever wanted, regardless of how long it takes. I cup one of her cheeks, leaning my forehead against hers. Rayanne leans into my space, pressing her lips firmly against mine. She doesn't linger long enough for me to thoroughly kiss her like I want. But that's a kiss made of promises of what's to come.

"Thank you," she whispers, wrapping her arms around my neck. "I'm sorry I don't know what the fuck I'm doing. I don't know how to live with all of these feelings inside of me right now. But I know you'll be there for me as I figure my shit out. The only thing I need is you waiting for me on my own time."

"I'm showing up," I promise. "Every day. Ray—"

She presses a finger to my lips, shutting me up. "I know." Rayanne removes her finger and dusts a feather light kiss on lips again. Then without a word, she climbs out of my lap and sits beside me. Rayanne plucks a Christmas tree cookie from the assortment and gathers a mini rainbow of colors for decorating. She nudges my knee with her own as she offers me a devilish smile.

Fuck.

This is happening.

acknowledgments

First and foremost, thank you to my readers for taking the time to read *The Trouble with Christmas*.

It takes a Writing Village to make any story a piece of work come to life, and I know I would have given up several times over, had I not had my group of friends helping me. To my Writing Village, including my Beta readers, ARC readers, Mae Harden, Maddi Bluhme, Rose Cedar, and Ellie Lukas.

There are a couple of people that have truly made this possible, and I need to give y'all a special shout out.

Caroline Corvin—Words cannot express how important you are to me. Thank you for always being so supportive and lending the shoulder needed most when I couldn't stand up on my own two feet. Your belief in my writing has centered and grounded me, making me think that I can actually do this crazy thing we call writing novels. My writing has become better because of our brainstorming and regular chatting.

Mekenzie Tarver—Girl, your enthusiasm for this writing project and making Caleb come alive is unparalleled. Thank you for your encouragement and guidance in creating characters like Caleb. And thank you for being there in the middle of the night when I woke up and needed someone to talk to. You have become a daily sounding board for ideas and brainstorming, and it's just so great having someone to talk to about writing whenever random thoughts filter through.

Many thanks to @bookishlybrilliant13, to whom I couldn't have made this second edition happen without you.

Thank you. <3

Lastly, thank you Louise Bay, Lauren Blakely, and Ivy Smoak. Y'all have all been inspirational to me. Without your written works, the words of kindness and encouragement, I don't think I'd have started down the path to write my own stories.

The Trouble with Christmas is officially book 1.5 in the True Heart Series, an interconnected five book series Loren is planning out. It begins with *Love in Plane Sight*, which is Isla and Graham's novel. This is currently being written as we speak.

Book two will be Caleb and Rayanne's full length novel and conclude their romance. Tropes include: The ex is back, suspenseful romance, no third-act break up, It was Always You

Book 3: Rosalyn and Chance's book, no title confirmed. Rosalyn is Graham's eldest sister. Tropes include Bad Boy/Good Girl, Enemies to Lovers, Forced Proximity, Broadway Musical setting, she's the new musical genius in town/he's broadway royalty, British MFC/American MMC

Book 4: Ellie and Reece's book, no title confirmed. Ellie is Graham's youngest sister. Tropes include Grumpy Dad/Sunshine Teacher, Age Gap, Second Chance Romance (for him), British MFC/American MMC

Book 5: Louise and Simon, no title confirmed. Louise is Graham's middle sister. Tropes include: mutual pining, older brother's best friend/younger sister, Supervisor/Co-worker romance, First love for both, handwritten notes, He reads romance novels, they're both scientists.

For more information, please check out her website or contact her through email.

about the author

Loren Sorensen is an emerging Contemporary and New Adult romance author based in Austin, Texas. A consummate word nerd, Loren has always been fascinated by finding the right words and storytelling. While she has been a lifelong writer, it wasn't until she became inspired to pursue her first series, the True Heart Series. The characters came to her in a dream, which was inspired by both her passion for romance and lingerie. Loren's first novella, *The Trouble with Christmas* is book 1.5 in the series and is available on Amazon.

When Loren isn't reading or writing, she collects tea like she collects books, is an amateur cook and baker, and loves exploring the world through her kiddo's eye.

facebook.com/lorensorensenwrites
instagram.com/lorensorensenwrites
tiktok.com/@lorensorensenwrites
goodreads.com/lorensorensen_writes